FIGHTING FOR CALLIOPE (POLICE SND FIRE: OPERATION ALPHA)

BADGE OF HONOR: TARPLEY VFD #3

HAVEN ROSE

Cover design: Buoni Amici Press
Edited by Gregory Alan

Dear Readers,

Welcome to the Police and Fire: Operation Alpha Fan-Fiction world!

If you are new to this amazing world, in a nutshell the author wrote a story using one or more of my characters in it. Sometimes that character has a major role in the story, and other times they are only mentioned briefly. This is perfectly legal and allowable because they are going through Aces Press to publish the story.

This book is entirely the work of the author who wrote it. While I might have assisted with brainstorming and other ideas about which of my characters to use, I didn't have any part in the process or writing or editing the story.

I'm proud and excited that so many authors loved my characters enough that they wanted to write them into their own story. Thank you for supporting them, and me!

READ ON!

Xoxo

Susan Stoker

LETTER FROM THE AUTHORS

To our amazing readers:

The Tarpley Volunteer Fire Department books have been a lot of fun for us to write, and we hope you enjoy them. Six talented authors came together to bring you these stories that take place in one small Texas town. With that in mind, please know that, although we tried very hard to consult with each other on details, there will be some minor differences in basic timelines, character portrayals, and storylines from book to book. While we take pride in our craft, it's almost impossible to have all the details match in six different works by six different authors, and we hope that you'll enjoy the uniqueness of each story rather than comparing them to each other. We ultimately wanted to bring you stories that you can enjoy, that will take you out of your world for a little while and drop you into another, and we know you'll appreciate them for the entertainment that they're intended to offer. Thanks for your support of us and happy reading!

~Silver, Deanndra, Haven, MJ, TL, and Nicole

ACKNOWLEDGMENTS

Acknowledgment and Dedication

My utmost thanks to Susan for inviting me to play in her world, and to Amy for being so helpful and willing to answer all the questions I asked of her.

Deanndra, MJ, Nicole, Silver, and TL, it was a pleasure. I look forward to working with you again. Drue, thank you for the wonderful graphics. They're gorgeous.

Readers, I hope you enjoy getting to know Tank, Calliope, and the other characters as much as I did. Perhaps you'll be seeing them again.

PROLOGUE

Tank

March…

I'm half-asleep, but quickly waking up. Then again, fire licking up the walls of your home can do that to you. Dad sounds calm, yet I can see the worry on his face. He's trying to hide it, though, not wanting any of us to realize the danger we're in. Carly and Bree come up behind me, their little hands shaking as they grip mine.

"Sherman, get your sisters outside," he commands as he wraps his arms around my mom and indicates for

me and my siblings to go first. I know then how serious this is simply because he didn't call me Tank. I'm not ashamed to admit I'm a bit scared by that fact, but I trust my dad to take care of us. He's never let me down.

We're standing on the sidewalk, shivering in our pajamas as the temperature has dropped, when my brain fully starts functioning again and I remember what's missing. Walking over to my dad, I nudge him to get his attention and tell him, "Sarah is inside," referring to the cat Bree got for Christmas. She loves that thing, and, when I hear her sobbing, I know she just realized none of us have her.

Dad tells me to watch over my mom and sisters, then goes back in. I want to beg him not to, something warning me I shouldn't let him go, but then I look at my youngest sister's face and her tears take the words right out of my mouth.

I know it's only been a few minutes since he walked away, though it feels like an eternity, but I'm so thankful when I hear the sirens getting closer. It doesn't take a genius to figure out our place is well beyond saving by this point.

We're all staring at the fire devouring our home, the sound louder than you'd think possible. Maybe it's because it's so quiet being this late at night, or perhaps a hush has fallen upon the whole town, as if all the resi-

dents are holding their breath, somehow knowing one of their own is in danger.

There's a creak, the wood groaning perhaps? I'm not sure, but I do know I don't like it. Sarah comes running out, headed in our direction, and I have to grab Bree as she starts to race forward. I make her stay there, promising I'll get her cat, then do just that, gathering Sarah in my arms and petting her, needing to reassure both of us, and check for injuries. She seems okay, and I breathe a sigh of relief at that discovery, but it fades instantly when I look at our door, and don't see my dad trailing after her.

Handing Sarah to Bree, I look at mom, then at the firefighters rushing to deal with the blaze, recognizing Dave, also a close friend of my dad's, from his size and walk. He has a swagger to him that's unmistakable, even now.

They talk amongst themselves very quickly, then split up, some going for the structure, others to hook up the hose and start spraying it. Mom moves closer to me, her arms encircling Carly and Bree, who is clutching Sarah tight, so I wrap mine around her. A glance at her expression informs me she knows it's bad, but hope hits nonetheless when Dave comes through the door, the shape of a man slung over his shoulder.

Paramedics hurry forward and Dave lays dad on a

stretcher, then removes his helmet, pain on his face, as they promptly place an oxygen mask on dad. He signals one of his men to join us, and, as if some kind of mental conversation passes between them, the firefighter leans close to mom and whispers in her ear.

"Girls, stay here, okay? I need to talk to Dave." They nod, the guy telling her he'll take care of them, then she takes my hand and has me go with her. Dave shakes his head, sadness in his eyes, and moves back a step. We're told it's critical he get to the hospital asap, and mom climbs in with him, then glances at me.

"Go," I urge, not wanting her to worry about us. "Someone will drive us there." And they do, though I can't remember who it is with all that's going on.

When we arrive, I tell them we're here for Otto Reardon and we're ushered to a room. Mom is standing next to the bed, tears trailing down her cheeks, dad's hand clasped in hers, her thumb stroking his wedding ring. She opens her mouth, and the words come at me as if we're in a tunnel, but I hear them regardless. Devastating news always finds a way to get through any barrier you try to erect to keep it out. She's telling us we need to let him go, that the doctors say he won't, can't, recover, his brain being deprived of oxygen too long, the smoke damage too severe.

I hate that my little sisters are hearing this, that I'm

failing at my job to always protect them, but I can't from this. And I'm the reason our dad is gone. If I hadn't mentioned the cat, he would've stayed with us. He'd be safe, making some lame joke to break the tension, to let us know it'll be okay because we have each other.

But it won't be, not ever again. And then the machines start beeping, people come rushing in, and I'd give anything to be on that bed instead of him.

When the doctor halts their efforts, my mom starts bawling, there's no other description for it, and he softly says, "Time of death..."

Gasping for breath, I shoot upright, my heart hammering in my chest as I wake. That was the worst night of my life, and whenever it haunts my sleep, I've learned it's a foreshadowing of sorts, a warning that something bad is coming. At least, that's been the case so far, a sign that things are about to change once again in some shape or form – Rosie's passing, the revelation of Carly's marriage and subsequent divorce, the fire we'd been called to assist with last month, and so on.

I can't help but question what it signifies now, not to mention wondering why the outcome is always the same, even though I know I'm dreaming and try to change it. I still lose my dad, still blame myself for it.

The only answer I've been able to come up with is the reality of that devastating evening is nightmare enough.

1

CALLIOPE

Spending time with Jemma over the weekend was exactly what I needed. We met in college, both attending the University of Oklahoma, my home state actually, to become teachers. With me being a little older, our bond is more like that of sisters, and I feel lucky to have her in my life. While we each earned our degrees, Jemma is the only one currently working in the field.

I, on the other hand, went in a completely opposite direction by chasing storms for a living. That might sound odd seeing as how I always expected to follow in my parents' footsteps as I saw the impact they had on others. While I enjoyed visiting various countries as a child, as I got older, I wanted a home base.

Which I found in college, and then one day between classes I met Brittney, who in turn introduced me to her friends – Lars, Oz, Shiro, and Wylder – and realized it was possible to have both a foundation and the adventure. It changed everything I thought I knew about myself, but I couldn't fully let go of my childhood dream of being an educator. So, I continued with that path, *and* took the fork in the road Brittney offered me. It was a lot of work, and delayed my graduation as I'd added years to my studies, but it was so damn worth it. Then, when Brittney and I met up again, the devastation of what happened in Moore having such a deep impact on all of us, we all knew we wanted to do something to prevent that from happening to others.

However, accomplishing your goals can come with a price, and I'm paying mine. Well, those who love me are. I know they worry about me, though none of them will outright ask me to stop doing this. But it's getting to me. I haven't been sleeping nor eating well. And my once rare migraines are coming on more frequently. I'm stressed over the secret I'm keeping from them, and I know it's impacting my already compromised system.

I could have, *should* have, shared this with Jemma when we were together, except I didn't want to ruin girl time. We don't get to do it often, but our schedules lined up thanks to a conference and we couldn't pass it up.

Plus, to be honest, her meeting that man at the bar, Short Shit, and yes, that made me giggle, also allowed me the opportunity to keep it to myself a little longer. It was a reprieve I gladly accepted. Besides, it's obvious there's something between them, the numerous back and forth glances proof of that. I finally pushed her to talk to him, dance with him. I don't know if there's anything to it other than a good time, but I'm hoping she'll take the risk to find out.

Now I'm back in Austin, in my room inside the antebellum we restored as a group. Again, another thing that took a lot of hours, curses, and learning, but, every time I see it, I know it was worth it.

When my phone rings, I reach out to grab it, pleased to see my brother's smiling face on the screen. "Little sis," Slade greets me, despite the fact he's not that much older than me. We're very close. Perhaps growing up as we did may have a had a lot to do with that as we were always the new kids wherever we went. We're both quiet, though he's more so. I've often asked myself why seeing as how dad and mom are very sociable, neither ever meeting a stranger.

"Big brother," I reply. He, too, abandoned the wandering lifestyle, sort of as his is just now done on two wheels with former veterans like himself. A few years after he enlisted, Slade's unit came under attack. He wasn't the only one injured, but his resulted in permanent nerve damage that ended his military career. He's a unique mix of badass and scholar, as we've termed him. His strength is not only physical, but mental as well, his brain capable of coming up with the great mysteries he publishes under the pen name Lawrence Slater. The last is close to Slade without being too obvious to hide his real identity. It was also my idea, so I might be partial to it.

"What's wrong?" He asks. How the hell does he always know? Trying to play it cool, I remind him I'm not one of his characters, but he calls me on my shit. "Cut it out." Knowing if I don't tell him, and somehow, he *will* know if I hold back, I tell him I've been debating resigning from the team, and that I know they'd like it if I did. "You have to do what makes *you* happy, not us. We're going to be concerned about your safety no matter what field you're in. It's what family does." With that reassurance, he drops the subject, promising to visit me soon. And reminding me to call dad and mom. They worry, you know. He's worse than they are. Walter and Winnie Lawrence are wonderful parents, very loving and affectionate with each other and their children, but they're also laid-back and prefer to go with the flow. You'd think that mindset would counteract their professions, but it makes them well-loved wherever they go.

I've noticed the others watching me with curiosity lately, as if they know I'm second-guessing myself. I don't mean that to sound harsh or judgmental, but what we do…there's a factor of strain involved, and if you don't find a way to relieve it that works for you, it can take a toll.

On the flip side, we can also do a lot of good. Our knowledge and focus on impending storms, keeping an eye on the potential path, and so much more can save lives by giving as much warning as possible.

I've always loved that part of it, and being able to do so with people I've grown close to makes it even better. Surprisingly, our videos have become quite popular. You wouldn't think so, or at least I wouldn't, but reality shows are huge, and this is pretty much the same thing.

I'm just not sure if this is the place for me anymore.

2

TANK

"You look like shit," Pops, or Dave as I knew him when I was younger, says as he steps into the bay where I'm currently reworking an engine. *Otto Repairs,* a play on my dad's first name as he loved puns, was his dream, and it almost died with him, but the residents of Tarpley, my hometown, and Bandera, where the shop is located, banded together until I was old enough, and ready, to take over the business. There are pros and cons to living in a small-town, but the good far outweighs the bad.

His greeting may sound rude to those who don't know him, but I do better than most. He cares about his people, as he calls those under his command. On top of that, we have a special bond as he and my dad were close, and he was there that night. His nickname is due to his addiction to Tootsie Pops, but it has a deeper meaning for me. He'll never replace my dad, nor has he ever attempted to, but he and I both know when I say Pops, I'm acknowledging his role in my life.

After losing my dad, we were not only homeless, but also overcome by grief, and Pops and his wife, Rosie, graciously offered us a place to stay on their ranch until Mom was ready to move forward. Understandably, it took a while, especially as she had to adjust to being a single mom of three and becoming the family's sole support.

During that time, he was patient with me, knowing my attitude was due to pain, and didn't hold it against me. Thank god. In between dealing with my dad being gone, I was doing everything I could to help mom with my sisters, as well as Rosie. Being there, with the work it entailed and the animals, was cathartic.

I started asking him all kinds of questions about joining the department, remembering how brave they were during the fire, the way they randomly checked on us afterward. Asking if they could do anything, offering to help at the garage, despite the lack of skills in that aspect. It was the thought that counted, and my mom and I appreciated it. They were a family, bonded by their dangerous job and the camaraderie that comes of it, but they also genuinely liked and respected each other.

"You come all the way out here," he chuckles since the drive is about fifteen minutes, "to insult me?" I ask him.

"Just calling it like I see it, and those bags under your eyes are getting heavy for even your big ass to carry around."

"Oh, you've got jokes now," I tease.

"Well, if the sasquatch fits…" We laugh at that, and I may casually flip him off, but it's all in good fun. Chatting for a few minutes, he circles back to why he came. I've told him before I relive that night, so he knows it's become an omen of sorts, and almost always, except in Erin's case, involves someone I know.

"I have no idea what it's trying to warn me. As far as I know, everyone is okay."

"Maybe it's no longer acting in that aspect." His tone lets me know he doesn't believe it either. "It was just the once, and nothing has gone down since?"

Shaking my head no, I admit why I appear

exhausted. I haven't sleep good in weeks. "I have it constantly now, and once I wake from it, I'm up. I can't close my eyes again." This is new territory to me, and I don't know how to deal with it except to power through it, as I have everything else that's come my way.

"Why don't you take a vacation?" He suggests, and that's not a bad idea. I can't remember the last time I took one. Oh, that's because I haven't. Hell, even if I don't go anywhere, but is time alone with my thoughts what I really need?

Nodding, knowing it's what he wants to hear, I say, "I just might do that."

"After the ceremony next month," he reminds me. Well, shit.

"You know I hate that kinda stuff."

"I do, but Conor and Erin will be there, and this means a lot to them. So, your anti-social self will have to suffer for a few hours. You can handle it."

"Trying to convince me or yourself?" I ask. He hates the attention, too. We all do, though I know we'll do it for them.

"Both," he replies and I grin at the confession. Pops hangs out for a bit, giving us time to catch up. Being volunteer firefighters, we all have full-time jobs, and, aside from meetings at the station, we aren't there often as fires thankfully aren't that common around here. Though, we do also help nearby areas when they need us, which is how we met Conor and Erin.

After he leaves, promises of dinner together soon made, we finish the jobs on today's schedule, then exchange chin lifts as we head to our respective vehicles. There are three of us, including myself. Maurice, or Mo as he prefers, lives here in Bandera while Leo is from Medina.

Mo has been here almost since the beginning, and is one of the main reasons the garage survived. He took over the day to day stuff, never pressuring me to step up until *I* let him know I was ready, and able, to. When I'd reached that point, he gave me a hug, said it's all mine, then happily went back to working on the vehicles. Dad trusted him implicitly, and so do I.

I hired Leo shortly after that, my first decision as a boss really, and I've never regretted it. Between him and Mo, I know the place is in good hands when I can't be here for whatever reason. There are some slow days simply because we're in and surrounded by small towns, yet business is pretty steady for the most part. Mom said Dad did a lot of research before choosing his location, and it's paid off.

Pulling in my driveway, I'm not surprised to see Bree's car, nor that she and my dog, Kevin, are outside playing. It's a weird name for a canine, I know, but it fits him.

"Dinner's on the stove," she informs me as Kevin rushes toward me. Okay, she also cooks enough for me when she's here to steal my food. I kneel, letting Kevin greet me as if I've been gone days, not hours. He's still a puppy age wise, but is already big because of his breed. Standing, I realize Bree is watching me pretty much the same way Pops had, Mo and Leo, too, now that I think about it.

It's not that I want anything bad to happen, but I'm between that proverbial rock and a hard place. If it does, I can finally sleep, except that means someone else's life has been impacted. That outcome versus me being tired? Yeah, I know which I'll choose. I'll just mainline coffee and take power naps in the interim.

The meal is delicious, as always, and I tell her she can break in every day as long as she feeds for me. "I have a key, dork," she reminds me with a fake glare.

"But did I give it to you?"

"Semantics," she retorts, then changes the subject by slipping Kevin a piece of steak, both then acting innocent when I raise a brow. Bree merely shrugs and gives him another. Kevin, I swear, smiles at me.

Later that night, I once more jolt awake, the dream lingering in my mind, I force my breathing to slow down, my heartbeat to calm, and wonder why, for the first time in twenty years, there was a noticeable change.

It wasn't a fire that forever disrupted my world, but a tornado, and my dad wasn't there. A woman, her face in shadows because of the darkened skies and the late hour, was reaching out for me, relying on me to save her, and I wanted to, more than anything. I somehow knew if I didn't, I'd regret it for the rest of my life, not that I'd have much of one without her in it.

The other obvious difference? I wasn't fifteen as I was then, but the age I am now, thirty-five, and I was fighting nature itself to get to her.

3

CALLIOPE

"Pack your bags and come see me for a while," Jemma says after we exchange greetings. I hate that I tense up when we talk because I love the woman like a sister. However, I know she's noticed a change in me, we've known each other too long for her not to, and I keep waiting for her patience to run out on me telling her why. And every conversation that ends with me not doing so makes me feel like a horrible friend.

"But it's storm season," I refute, admittedly it's half-hearted as I suddenly very much want to go see her.

"And we both know you can take some time off. Please." Jemma sighs the last part, and there's so much concern in it that my heart twists. Is the rush of what I do, the possibility of helping others, really worth the worry I cause those who care about me? That's a question I've been asking myself a lot lately. "You know how I told you our volunteer fire department helped that woman? Well, there's gonna be a thank you party of sorts next month for them. I'd like you to come." I ask for specifics and she lets me know it won't be anything outrageous, but there will be a small ceremony and a fair. "Perhaps a speech or two, some games and booths. I think we'll get a chance to dunk a few of the guys."

"How can I say no to that?" I joke, but honestly, I don't think I can. I could use a little break. Maybe it'll give me a chance to get my head on straight and help me figure out what I want to do. It's not fair to myself or the team to stay in this mental limbo.

"And you can help me with Aunt Eden's house," she states, the pain of losing her still as clear in her voice as if it was yesterday. Understandable considering her aunt raised her after she lost her dad. My girl can't seem to catch a break. Unless...

"Talk to...okay, I can't call him that name... Have you spoken to him?" I admit, which makes her laugh, exactly the reaction I was hoping for.

After meeting Jemma, I could really no longer tease Slade about his older sibling protectiveness over me, though I still did, of course, because she brings that same instinct out in me.

"My lips are sealed. You'll have to get that out of me in person."

"That's dirty pool." I pretend to sniffle, then tell her I couldn't be prouder of her guilt trip. I agree to let her know after I double-check some things, wondering if the others would like to go as well since a vacation of any length, even a weekend, here and there helps people reset. When the doorbell rings, I rush downstairs, curious who it could be since I don't think we're expecting anyone.

Surprised to see a delivery driver, I sign for the package and close the door behind me, locking it once more because you can never be too safe. I groan when I see the return address is Slade's, knowing his sense of humor can be out there. Then again, so can mine.

Sis,

. . .

I heard lavender is supposed to be calming and shit, so here.

Me

Opening it, I laugh when I see various items in that scent. A candle, lotion, shampoo, conditioner, and, oh man, he didn't. Essential oil. We used to always tease our mom about her fascination with the stuff, but we couldn't deny it worked more often than not. Lifting it from the box, I find another note, this one folded so it was hidden underneath, with a smiley face drawn on top. Of course, there's also a tongue sticking out of it. The jerk.

I knew you'd pick this one up first. You just couldn't resist. In all seriousness, it is supposed to help you sleep and fight migraines. So, use it.

Love you.

. . .

He really is the best, though I won't admit it to him, and the tightness in my chest isn't only from his thoughtfulness. I wasn't lying about the lack of sleep and headaches; I just wasn't entirely truthful either.

Twisting the cap, I take a whiff of it and let the smell swirl around me, a sense of nostalgia for simpler times when we were kids and seemed to have no worries. I silently hope it works some magic on my state of mind. If it does, it'll be a miracle, and it's beginning to feel like that's exactly what I need.

4

CALLIOPE

April…

The closer we got to Tarpley, the calmer I felt, the quieter I became. It made no sense, but that's exactly what happened. The others, the whole team coming with me as I'd hoped, talked amongst themselves, wondering what the town was like and sharing jokes. I chimed in from time to time, but it didn't escape my notice the questioning glances I'd been getting for a while weren't occurring as often as they did back home.

When we arrived, everyone jumped out the second the vehicle stopped, eager to stretch our legs and breathe some fresh air. The distance from each other isn't bad either, a few of us had teased. We're all staying at the B&B, but I went to the fair early to meet Jemma for lunch before the ceremony.

The conversation flowed easily, as always, between us. It doesn't matter if it's been hours, days, weeks, or months since we've each other, we pick up as if no time had passed. And every visit always makes me realize how much I miss her when we aren't together.

Now I'm sitting beside her, listening to Erin Gardner talk about how scary it was to be at the mercy of the wildfire, her boyfriend, Conor Paxton, offering support when the emotions overcome her, fear in his eyes at the memory of almost losing her. My heart hurts for them as I imagine what they must've been feeling, and I agree when those being honored are referred to as heroes. And while everyone is focusing on all of them, my eyes haven't left the man labeled Tank. That's probably not polite as this is a serious matter, but so is the way I'm reacting to him.

He's…a lot. I've never been afraid of a challenge and my gut is telling me breaking through his defenses might be my greatest one yet. My body jolts when Jemma gently elbows me, and I quickly look her way and find her giving me a grin. Yeah, she noticed me noticing him. Damn, that sounds so high schoolish, but I can't deny the freaking butterflies in my stomach. I used to feel them when we were chasing or tracking a storm, so I know what they signify. Anticipation, adrenaline, and nerves all rolled into an almost overwhelming ball of emotions. However, I've discovered over the years I tend to thrive on it. A fact that has derailed any relationship I've attempted, so I stopped trying long ago.

Perhaps I hadn't met the man that understood that rush, not only from the potential danger, but helping people, sometimes literally being what saves them. It's not that we're playing God, we never could nor would I want to, and to those who aren't in particular fields, that thought might sound cocky, but it couldn't be farther from the truth. Storms, fires, and so on are evidence of how vulnerable we all are, and that we must rely on one another in times of need.

The crowd breaks out in applause, those on stage appearing uncomfortable with the thanks they're being given for doing their jobs. Once the crowd disperses to enjoy the fair the town has set up, Jemma and I part ways, her to talk with Angel as it's obvious they have some things to discuss, and me to wander. And I'm sure Brittney is trying to cope with the fact Dirty-D is here, something that shocked the hell out of me when I saw him. To say they have a lot to discuss is an understatement, and I send a quick mental 'good luck' to them both. They'll need it.

Patting my pocket, I make sure I have the required accessories, fully aware I need to come clean soon. Hell, I don't know how I've been able to keep it hidden as long as I have. I can't even say it might be luck as I haven't felt anything but the bad kind surrounds me since this started. That cliché about a decision having the ability to change everything? It's true. Turning left instead of right during my usual jog one day had lasting and potentially life-threatening repercussions. But I can't let the panic take me as to what their reactions may be or the risks to my health that I now face on a daily basis. Taking short breaths, I reach into my purse and clutch my safety net in case I can't get this under control before it's too late.

Forcing myself to calm down, I try to focus on something else, and my gaze unerringly finds Tank...in a dunk tank, no less. Is it even big enough to hold him? The man is at least six and a half feet of pure muscle. Will it create a tidal wave if the young girl winding up to throw the ball hits her target?

I laugh when I realize he's egging her on. And, from I can make out as I slowly move closer to watch, she has a wicked arm, one that numerous softball coaches would love to have on their team according to a couple of the men nearby. I watch as she scuffs the grass underneath her foot, appearing satisfied when she finds dirty. My concentration is entirely on her, the anticipation almost visible in the gathering crowd. I focus on her, but as she lets go of the ball, it moves too fast for me to keep track of it until I hear a thwack, immediately followed by the sound of her victim, for that's surely what he is, falling in the water.

"Damn straight I throw like a girl," she declares smugly as she walks away, a sputtering Tank congratulating her as his buddies tease him. He takes it all in stride, not in the least upset a teenager got the better of him.

He stands, blond hair darker now that it is wet, drenched cutoffs showcasing interesting places as the water highlights others, and I step forward with a towel that'd been out of his reach. Which says a lot as the man has a wingspan that could rival that of the wandering albatross.

Thankfully, that thought, one of those weird pieces of information I learned from my parents that stuck in my brain and reappears at random times, was not verbally said, just mentally. It's made for some awkward conversations.

When he takes it, his fingers brushing mine, a shiver courses through me despite the heat in the air, and his reaction shows that he felt it, too. He quickly dries off, then pulls on a shirt, socks, and shoes, then introduces himself.

"Tank," he says, holding his now dry hand out as he gives me a grin that somehow comes off boyish when he's anything but, and adds, "though I'm thinking you already know that." I laugh, telling him I do, but it's a pleasure to officially meet him. His response melts my heart because smart men are my weakness, and add that to what I've already seen and heard about him? I'm toast. "Likewise."

"I'm Calliope," I inform him, knowing there's two pronunciations of it, so I always make sure to introduce myself using my full name when I meet new people. My parents chose kuh·lai·uh·pee because of the meaning behind it and the circumstances of my birth. As much as I love it, and the reason for it, it gets mixed reactions.

Tank, and perhaps it's because he goes by that, merely nods. "I like it. You don't hear it oft…ever," he corrects himself, making me smile. "Something tells me you're just as unique as it is." The look in his green eyes when he says it…yeah, that's not a line. He means it, and I thank him with a blush.

"Coming from a man named Tank?" He chuckles, the sound echoing through me.

"There's a story behind that," he assures me, then winks as he adds, "and not the one you'd think."

"Do I get a hint?" I ask, shocked I'm flirting. I don't do that. But it seems I'm suddenly willing to change my usual way of doing things for him.

Now he appears a bit bashful, admitting, "My dad was a history buff."

I see the pain on his face, especially at the use of the past tense, but I don't comment on it, instead focusing on the rest to not make it harder on him. "I'm guessing you were a big baby," he smirks at how that sounds, "when you were born, but that's not why." With a "hmmm," I tap my finger on my chin, exaggerating my thinking to lighten the mood, and try to recall history lessons from my parents. I'm drawing it out on purpose, giving him time to regroup, and thankfully, it's working. The teasing light in his gaze is back, as is smugness, but he's about to be disappointed. He has no idea who he challenged. "Sherman." His jaw drops in shock, letting me know I'm right. And I can't help but give a little happy dance, as in stomping my feet as I spin in a circle, then high-five myself. He throws his head back and laughs, yet there's a rustiness to it, which makes me sad. I'm not done, though. "I almost went with Tecumseh as it was named by the British after William Tecumseh Sherman, an American Civil War general, but I hedged my bets." Instead of the dazed look that most get when I start going, he appears fascinated. He walks around me, then shakes his head when he's once more in front of me. "What?"

Tank shrugs, "Just trying to figure out where you store all this information." I giggle at his silliness. "You have facts like that at the ready all the time?"

"My parents are teachers. We traveled all over as the world was their classroom."

"We?"

"The four of us. I have an older brother, Slade."

"So, unique names run in the family."

"My parents, Walter and Winnie, would disagree."

"Honestly, mine had every intention of me going by my given name, but dad was watching a documentary one day about tanks, when," he quickly glances around and points at a young woman with the same color hair, "that brat, aka my youngest sister, Bree, who was all of four, heard the narrator say Sherman. She turned and saw a picture of a Sherman tank on the screen and said, "Brudder." I'm bent over laughing, but it's too much for my body and I feel the tightness in my chest and press my hand to it, as if I can force air into my lungs. Please not here. Not now. Without making a big deal, Tank takes my arm and hurries us to a different area. "Where's your rescue inhaler, sweetheart?" I reach into the side of my purse and take it out. Like he knows I don't want people to see, he stands, blocking out any chance of that happening, and patiently waits as I use it, counting to see how long until it takes effect. Once I know it's working, hating that he saw me at my weakest, embarrassment hits and I try to hide, but I don't have a chance to run, well, briskly walk away as I'm still a little limited, before he whispers, "Don't go. Please."

We stand there, staring at each other, and I realize his hand slid down to grip my own, and I find his thumb caressing the back of it in a soothing manner. I concentrate on it and it allows me to fully regain control of my breathing. "Thank you," I say just as quietly as he'd spoken, irrationally feeling as if the bubble around us will burst if I don't.

"You good?" Nodding, I stand straighter, mourning the loss of his touch as his hand drops, take a deeper breath than I'd been able to a mere few minutes ago, and put my inhaler away. I also do so a little slower than necessary, giving myself a bit to regroup.

When I ask how he knew, he confesses, "Bree and I might've watched a few episodes of a medical show she liked. Some stuff stuck."

"Some?" I question, appreciating that he's taking all of this in stride.

"All right. It was a couple months ago and we binged it."

"Then I'll have to thank your sister." I start to apologize, realizing how forward that might sound, but he doesn't give me chance. Instead, he brushes a strand of black hair behind my ear and tells me I'll have plenty of time to do just that. A fact that makes me extremely happy because it's evidence that he's feeling this, too.

"Would you be my date for the fair?" He asks.

"I'd love to."

"What would you like to see?"

"If I answered all of it would that seem greedy?" He laughs, telling me no, and he'd happily show me every inch. The little devil on my shoulder urges me to question if we're still talking about the fair, but I shush it, telling it to behave…for now.

Tank

I wish Conor and Erin hadn't been in danger, but it is essentially the reason this special woman and I met. For that, I'm thankful. "What brought you to Tarpley?"

"One of my favorite people live here."

Jokingly I say, "But we just met, so that means there's two of us here."

"You're a funny man."

"Quite a few would disagree with you."

"Everyone has their own definition, neither is

wrong." I nod, acknowledging that, and she informs me, "Jemma Haner."

"How do you two know each other?"

"College."

"That's right, she left for a couple years. Oklahoma, wasn't it?"

"Yeah. My home state. Her and I both went for teaching."

"You're a teacher?"

"My degree says so," she grins, though I have a feeling that's as much as she wants to share about it. Crazy me, I pick another she might want to avoid while taking her hand in mine.

"So, Jemma doesn't know? Your family either?" I don't mention what I'm referring to as I don't need to.

"No." Her reply is that simple, and complicated. Perhaps this isn't the place to discuss something so serious, but maybe that's why we should. This is a celebration of life, of community, and I'm thinking she needs to see that things aren't always as dire as they seem. I'm not saying I can save her, nor that she needs or wants me to, but perhaps we can save each other. "Can I ask why?" When I glance at her, she's grinning, and, knowing how I'd react to that,

I instantly tack on, "And don't say I can, but you might not answer."

"Already have me pegged as a smartass?"

"Takes one to know one," I admit.

"Or you have experience because of Bree?"

"That, too. As well as my other sister, Carly."

"Oh man, you against two of them? That had to be torture..." I start to nod, allowing a look of defeat on my face, only to learn she tricked me, "for them." And then she actually starts to scamper away, though I quickly reach out to stop her. I swear she mutters something about a wingspan, so I have to question her on it. I knew I was attracted to her, but when she tells me what she said, that's when I realize this is so much more than I suspected. And that scares me. Not because of what might, *will,* happen between us, but that the idea of losing her at some point already hurts. That's an inevitable fact of life, we're only given so many days, and some, tragically, have few than others. What if she's in the latter group?

If the ache of that reality is the case following a couple hours in her company, how the hell did mom go on after only having seventeen years with dad? Part of me wants to run, to try to forget how good being with her feels, but I've never been a coward.

"Tank?" I hear her, yet I can't respond. I'm trapped in memories, guilt, and I can't help but wonder if I'm a coward after all. For I do the only thing I can to protect myself…

I walk away.

5

TANK

I don't even know why I came in. I'm pretty much useless today as I once more didn't sleep, dreaming yet another night. But the end changed again, the woman's face now visible, and I realized it had been Calliope the whole time. Unfortunately, I walked away from her a second time, and I'd instantly turned back, knowing I'd chosen incorrectly, but she was gone. That more than the dream kept me up long before the sun rose, and it still haunts me hours later. As does the knowledge my dad would be ashamed of me.

"What the fuck is wrong with you?" Pops greets me the second he sees me. This time, unlike the other visit, his tone lets me know he is *pissed.*

Shrugging, I attempt cluelessness. “Slept wrong. Does that count?”

“Don’t get cute, son.” Shit. “I’m disappointed in you.” That calls for an additional shit with a fuck thrown in.

“To be honest, I’m disappointed in myself,” I admit.

“I saw you with her, you know?” I look at him, wondering exactly what he saw because Pops doesn’t miss much. “You gonna make me get all feely?” Then he sighs, stares directly into my eyes, and states, “I’ve known you a long time, Sherman. I’ve always been proud of you, until yesterday.” I open my mouth, but he stares at me, informing me in a gruff tone, “I’m not done,” and I instantly snap it shut. “That woman made you *feel* something other than hatred for yourself for the first time in two freakin’ decades.” I can’t hide my shock from that news. “You think I don’t know that about you? I knew it then and I’ve known it every day since. But from the instant you saw her, and yes, I was watching. Of course, I was. I know I’m not your father, have never tried to be, but that doesn’t mean I don’t love you like one – your whole countenance changed when your eyes landed on her. I think the whole damn town felt it. ” I want to tease him, to deflect his attention from me, but I listen instead. My respect for him demands it even if he doesn't verbally request it.

"The way she made me feel scared me."

"That scares you, yet you run into burning buildings? Yes, it's a job, but it's also a calling for you. Your dad was one of the best men I've ever known, and his loss is never unnoticed. But I have two questions for you." And then he puts things in perspective as only a man with his wisdom, his own personal loss, can, "First, if he was still here, how many people would've died or suffered horribly because you weren't there to save them? Second, why do you refuse to reach out and let someone help you?" My head drops, shame weighing it down, and just when the silence begins to be too much, I feel him sit beside me, then he says, "Your mom and I have talked about the pain of losing a spouse, but even if we hadn't, I could tell you without any doubt if we'd gone into our respective marriages knowing how tragically and soon they'd end, we still would've made the same decision to tie our lives with them. You know why? We treasure the time we had with them, not what we didn't. *That's* what is important."

Calliope

I still have no idea what happened. Things were going great between us, or so I thought, but he left me standing there, staring after him as I tried to pull myself together and act as if I didn't want to cry. Which was weird considering we really didn't even know each other. But it hurt, not only him apparently being able to so easily leave, but the realization of what could've been had he not.

I'd stopped looking too far in the future, unsure of exactly how long of one I had as I was still coming to terms with my new normal, but Tank made me eager to see what it had in store for me, for us. That hope is still there, something telling me to not give up completely. Yet as the hours passed, as the sun set and rose again this morning, an occurrence I saw as the inability to fully breathe once more woke me from the endless tossing and turning, it began to fade.

Perhaps the reality of what spending time with me could mean because of my asthma took a while to hit him, and when it did, he couldn't, or didn't want to, deal with it? I wouldn't think that'd bother a firefighter, but seeing life-threatening situations professionally is a whole lot different than accepting one in your personal life, so it's possible.

At least I made use of all those hours I couldn't sleep, which gave me the ability to make decisions about my path, and where I want it to lead. Honestly, even without the medical issues, I'm no longer sure chasing storms is what I want to do. Oh, it's still exciting, and makes a difference in the lives of others, but I'd vowed to myself to find a home base, to stop traveling, and while I did the first in a way, I hadn't the second.

Our house has pieces of all of us in it, yet that's all they are. Pieces. It's not entirely any of ours, and while we've become a family over the years, it isn't the same as *having* one. As in, a husband, children. A dog or cat. Thankfully, I'm not allergic to either of those, so I can have both if I wanted. And I do. However, I can't if I'm on the road more often than I'm home.

So, I got out my laptop and took a chance, telling myself if I found a listing for this area or close to it, it was a sign that my place is here. Sure enough, a position for an elementary school in Pipe Creek was available. The posting stated it's temporary with an option to become permanent. I don't know the circumstances surrounding the former teacher leaving, not that I need to as long as it doesn't have any bearing on the next person who takes the job, and applied for it. I'd attached the resume I keep somewhat updated after making a few changes, and the information they required to ensure my certification was current, which it is. I may not use it, but I like knowing I can if I ever want to. Hitting send, peace had settled over me, and I knew then I'd made the right decision for me.

I'm not telling Jemma yet, though. She'll get her hopes up, and mine already are enough for the both of us. If I hear back from them I will, unless it goes nowhere.

Finishing my Earl Grey, I grab my crossbody purse and take a quick peek inside to double-check my stuff is all there, then throw away my now empty cup.

Spending a few hours with Jemma will be fun, and, unless I miss my guess, I bet I'll be seeing Angel, too. I hope so. She sounded happy when she talked about him, well, before she learned what he was keeping from her. I understand her being mad and hurt because of it, but love changes things.

And it's not like I can point fingers at him for not telling her right away when I'm not being entirely truthful either. Perhaps I want her to forgive him as it means she might do the same for me.

Yeah, they're gonna be just fine. After spending a few hours with Angel and Jemma, I have no doubt they'll make it. His presence kept her from asking questions I wasn't sure I was ready to answer, and made the fact I only took a sip or two of the beer he gave me easier to hide. Alcohol is not good with my health issues, but since she doesn't know about that yet…ugh. I need to woman up and just spit it all out.

I also might've been constantly checking my phone, which she did notice, but once again, thank you, Angel. I almost squealed when I got a response to my application, and made my exit without being too obvious about it. I don't know if fate is smoothing the way for this all to happen, or this area is sorely in need of people in my field, but they asked me to come in for an interview. Packing for numerous possibilities is smart, which means my suitcase is never lacking at least one dressy outfit, so at least I'm prepared for that. If I need more, I'll deal with that then.

Not long after returning to my room, I'd called Jemma to let her know I wouldn't make it to dinner. Plus, I had been ready to talk, if Angel wasn't attached to her face that is. They're sickeningly sweet, but she's also really the only one I know in any kind of relationship aside from my parents.

"Can you talk for a minute?" I asked her. She must've heard the seriousness in my tone because she told Angel I needed her and a door shut shortly after that. I told her what happened with Tank, and she was quiet for a minute, then wanted to know if he'd told me anything about his family. "Some, but I got the feeling it made him sad, so I steered the conversation in a different direction," I'd responded.

"You can't live here and not know everyone's business," she'd reminded me, then softly said, "so trust me when I say you need to hear it from him." I'd made a harrumph in disbelief, according to her, because she'd added, "From what you shared, and I know you aren't the type to embellish, he likes you. A lot. And that, factored with what I know, means

I can state with almost complete confidence, you scared him."

"The man's name is Tank."

"Yeah, so?"

"Uhh, I thought my question was self-explanatory," I'd answered, not sure why she'd been confused.

"Fear comes in all sizes, and for various reasons, Callie," she'd calmly told me, her teacher voice ringing through loud and clear. Then again, yeah, it had been a lesson I needed to hear, and she wasn't done. "You only have half the story, my friend." I hate that she knows more about him than I do. Not because I'm jealous of her knowing him all this time, and I know it's only been as fellow residents, but I want to have a long history with him, which is stupid considering we don't have a present.

I push our earlier conversation from my mind when there's a knock, and sit there a minute, debating on if it's familiar or new, which is now the stupidest thing I've ever done. Forget my thought of just seconds ago.

Literally shaking my head at myself, I open the door, and quickly drop the polite smile I instantly aimed at the person on the other side. I shouldn't be this happy to see him. I want to make a snide remark, but his expression steals all my thunder. It's obvious he didn't fare well either since we parted. Yeah, we'll go with that label for what he did.

"Five minutes. Please."

"You really don't owe me anything," I tell him. "We're strangers."

He invades my space at that. "Neither of us believe that." I can't deny that, so I step back and allow him inside. His gaze immediately hones in on my luggage, and his entire demeanor changes. "You're leaving? Just giving up on us without even giving us a chance to see what we could be?" Is he freaking kidding me?

"I'm not, and you already did that for us."

His shoulders slump, and he plops on the bed, head in his hands. "I'm an ass," he admits. "I'm sorry, again. I would like to talk to you, though, and while it doesn't excuse my behavior, it might explain it." I don't know what makes me do it, other than I want to be near him, but I sit beside him. He's watching me so closely, as if everything hinges on my answer, so I nod. Am I too much of a chickenshit that I can't even *say* yes? Tank must be wondering the same thing because he doesn't immediately start, but continues to stare at me.

"Yes. I need to hear it."

"First, I want to ask you to not think less of me, which is hard to do considering I was a coward yesterday." He snorts, then adds, "Ironic as I was being honored for my heroics, huh?"

"Coming here took a lot of courage," I inform him sincerely, "and, as this is clearly hard for you to talk about, coward is the last term I'd use for you." Tank reaches over and takes my hand, and I'm not sure if it's his way of thanking me for what I said or if he needs the support he feels I can offer.

"My dad's name was Otto, and I'm the reason my mom is a widow, and my sisters are orphans. Bree barely remembers him because she was only five." Then he proceeds to tell me about the fire, his description so real I feel like I'm there myself, fear gripping me as he continues, and when he's done, his voice is thick with emotion. "I sent him back in there. I killed him." Tipping his face to me, no longer able to take not seeing it, I swear I hear a crack in the center of my chest as it breaks at sight of the tracks on his cheek. This man, for as big as he is, his heart is even more so. But the burden he mistakenly placed on his own shoulders at such a young age has weighed him down for far too long. And, without it needing to be said, I now know why he left as we were getting to know each other. Jemma was right, sort of. It's not that I scared him, but that allowing me to get too close did.

"As did Bree, since it was her cat, your parents' for buying Sarah, your mom and Carly for letting him go, and your dad for going."

"That's not true," he shouts.

"Then why is it for you?" I quietly ask him. "You just noticed she was missing first."

"And told him."

"Because he's your dad," and I used the present tense intentionally. "He taught the three of you that you could always go to him with a problem, right?" Tank nods. "It's what parents do. He sounds like a wonderful man and father, which means he wouldn't have let anything stop him from doing whatever he could to make your family happy."

"If I didn't know any better, I'd swear you and Pops planned this. He's tried to convince me to let go of my guilt, too."

"This Pops is a wise man," I tease, though there's truth to it.

"I'm glad he didn't hear that," he jokes, then

turns serious. "He told me that if we hadn't lost my dad, I might not have joined the department."

"Is he correct?"

"All I ever wanted to do was grow up to be like my dad, to work at the garage, and eventually take over."

"And?"

"To quote Meat Loaf, 'two out of three ain't bad.'"

"So, you didn't take over the garage yet?" I ask, purposefully choosing it to make the others true. He looks at me in shock, then realizes what I'm saying.

"You biased where I'm concerned?"

"Maybe, but it doesn't make my opinion any less true."

He breezes over that and admits, "I feel closer to my dad when I sit at his desk, work in the same bays he did, see his name on the sign. Between the shop and the station, I have very little free time," – Is he warning me? – "and what I do have is precious, reserved for my family."

"And what do you do for yourself?" His silence is answer enough. "I admire your dedication and devotion to honoring his memory by taking care of your loved ones, as well as people you know *and* those you don't. But who takes care of you? You need to let someone in."

"I don't know how."

"Me either," I confess, "so how about we learn together?"

Tank

Relief like I've never experienced rushes through me at her question because it tells me I didn't screw up. Okay, I did, but not beyond redemption. "Those are perhaps the greatest words I've ever heard."

When she laughs at what I meant as a compliment, I'm a bit confused. "Sorry. That was the sweetest thing anyone has ever said to me."

"Then why was it funny?"

"Do you know what my name means?"

"She was a Greek muse, I believe."

"Yes, ironically enough of heroic poetry," she states with a wink at me. "Which means I'm fully qualified to say, I meant this wonderful man by the name of Tank, that this couple wanted to thank."

That makes me groan, but it lightens the mood as we both needed. Getting back to her story, she tells me, "It literally translates to beautifully-voiced. From what my parents told me, mom's pregnancy with me was difficult toward the end, and there were complications when I was born. They eagerly awaited my cry, but as the minutes passed, their excitement turned to fear. The nurses were rushing around, their hushed tones conveying something was wrong with me all the while pretending it wasn't. Thankfully, one of the women, whom they later learned was of Greek descent, refused to give up and honestly, she saved me. When I finally cried, dad said she whispered, 'There you go, Calliope. I knew you could do it.' Then they asked her to repeat it and the meaning of it..."

"And they picked it because they were terrified they'd never hear yours."

"Exactly. Over the years, people have shortened it to Callie, and I don't mind, but my full name means a lot to me because of the story behind it, and it's all my parents use. My brother goes back and forth, depending on the situation or his mood."

"It suits you perfectly."

"Thank you," she responds. "That irony you mentioned earlier?" I nod. "Did you know in nineteen forty-four a new tank made its first appearance in France?"

"I did not, but I'm glad you do. I like your knowledge drops." She smiles, her hazel eyes shining from pleasure at that, and it makes me wonder if they aren't always well-received. "What was it called?"

"The T34, or Sherman Calliope." I burst out laughing, but my heart is soaking it all in, telling fate it's listening. That I know she's mine.

"What are the odds?"

"One out of impossible?"

"Seems as if we'd be thumbing our nose at that if we didn't take it as a sign."

"And it's not the first since coming here. Hell, it started on the drive over."

"They haven't all read "yield" or "danger," have they?"

"What if I told you it's more like "one way"?

"What if I told you as long as it leads to me, I'm happy?"

"I think it just might." Then she looks at her suitcase and informs me, "I was set to leave with my friends, but I had a lot of time to kill last night."

"I'm..."

"Don't. I understand, truly. And maybe we each needed the opportunity to realize we had a decision to make. I used it to think about what I wanted to do next. I told Brittney and the others I'm staying, and they support me in that. They've known I haven't been myself for a while, and might've even seen this coming before I did." And she tells me about the position she put in for, the interview she's going on for it, and I want to shout at the news. "I need to figure out where I belong."

"Will you give me a chance to show you it might be in Tarpley?"

"That was my wish, but wasn't sure if that's what you wanted."

"So you're staying here?" I stupidly ask, even though she's all but said so.

"Well, not here as I only had the room for a few days."

"Can't you extend it?"

"I'm planning on it. However, I'm going to see if there's a cheaper room. It's not that I can't afford this one," the prices here tend to be very reasonable, "but I was raised to be frugal."

"This may be too early to ask this; however, do you trust me?" She nods, and I hope I'm not rushing her, while also knowing we may only have so much time together depending on the outcome of her interview. "First, you allergic to dogs?" When she answers no, and that she's always wanted a pet, I know I have a secret weapon and I am not afraid to use it. "You can stay with me as long as you want." I vote for forever. "I have a spare room," I quickly reassure her just to be safe.

"I don't want to put you out or anything."

"It's a win all the way around. It's free, you need a bed, I live alone and have the space, and it'll give us a chance to explore this thing between us."

"Why'd you ask about dogs?" That isn't a no.

"Kevin."

"Michael." When I peek at her in confusion, she responds, "I thought we were tossing out names," and wanted to play, too.

"Well, now I'm wondering why you picked that one," I mutter. Damn straight I'm jealous at how quickly she used it. Her smirk at my obvious reaction taunts me to have another, and I seal my lips to hers. Thankfully, she seems to like this one because I feel her start to lower her body to the mattress, and pull me with her. Propping myself above her with one arm to keep my weight off her, I cup the back of her head and angle it to the right.

With a nip to her fuller bottom lip, she opens as I anticipated she would, allowing me to fully taste her.

I don't know how long we explore one another's mouths, but I could do it for hours and still want more. Reluctantly parting, her sound of regret at doing so matches mine, and I'm tempted to connect us once more, until I feel her hand slip under the hem of my shirt

And when she drags her fingers upward, the nails lightly digging into my skin, I have to force myself not to spill in my jeans. It's been forever for me and nothing could compare to the impact this woman has on me even if it hadn't.

As badly as I want to bury myself in her, I'm not sure we're ready for that step. I tell her so, to which she agrees, but her wink steals a piece of me when she adds, "Although, we can still have some fun."

"That we can," I state, "after you tell me about the Michael thing."

Calliope, because that's how I see her now, puts me out of my misery and informs me, "It's my dad and brother's middle name."

"You're going to keep me on my toes, aren't you?"

"Probably," she replies with sass.

"I'm okay with that as it means you're keeping me." After a hard kiss, I stand and reach my hand out to help her do the same. "Let's grab your stuff and get home." Yes, I referred to it that way because I want her to start thinking of it as such. "Do you have a car here?"

She shakes her head. "I rode with the others."

"Can I apply to be your chauffeur?" I joke.

"I might need to see some references." Taking my cell from one of my rear pockets, I use my index finger to unlock it and give it to her.

"If you go to my favorites, you'll find them." She's hesitant to look, but I urge her to, wanting her to know she truly can trust me and I don't intend to have any secrets between us. Calliope can have the damn code to my phone if she wants, not that I'd ever give her any reason to doubt me where she's concerned.

She does as I suggested, and reads them off. "Mom. Carly. Bree. Shop. Pops. What's the name of the garage?"

"I told you my dad's name."

"Otto."

"Dad had a great sense of humor, and loved puns." When she starts cracking up a minute later,

I recall yesterday's scare and instantly prepare to get her inhaler, now that I know where she keeps it. Thankfully, it's not needed. "Please let me be right," she fervently wishes, then offers, *"Otto Repairs?"* How did she? "Puns are everything," she informs me. "If you have shirts, I will gladly wear one because that is hilarious."

She seems so excited, I hate to tell her we don't, unless… "They're only for employees." Calliope takes my hand and starts pulling me, well, trying to, toward the door.

"What's with the sudden rush?"

"I can't snag one of yours if I'm not at your place now, can I?"

"Muse, you can have any damn thing of mine you want." She's already stolen more than half my heart, and I know the rest will soon follow.

6

CALLIOPE

I love Tank's home. It's everything I always pictured my own being. And Kevin, well, I've claimed him as mine, or he did that to me. He's a gorgeous golden retriever that loves to be petted and to cuddle. When Tank had walked me to my room, we'd exchanged a passionate kiss, one that tempted me to follow him to his, and Kevin had looked between the two of us. I swear he was debating which to spend the night with, but Tank told him to stay with me, and he did.

Right now, my hand is gently stroking his fur as I attempt to get my breathing under control. When I woke, Kevin's head was on my arm, like he knew I was struggling and was offering comforting without putting weight on the troubled area.

Always prepared for this inevitability, I scoop what I need off the nightstand and wait for it to take effect. Kevin's eyes are on me the whole time, and when I stand, he's right beside me, silently letting me know I'm not alone.

Padding on bare feet to the door, I quietly open it, not wanting to disturb Tank as it's after midnight. Taking him at his word of making myself at home, I head to the kitchen to grab a glass of water, hoping by the time I'm done drinking it, I'll be able to go back to sleep.

Twenty minutes later, Kevin and I reverse our steps, but we don't make it to our destination. I'd paid attention to which room was Tank's, and as we get closer to it, Kevin starts whining. I'm not comfortable turning the knob to let him inside, but he refuses to budge when I attempt to continue to my door.

Retracing my steps, I bend down to...I don't know, see if I can somehow convince Kevin I can't give him what he wants. When I do, he grows quiet like he's listening, though he's not moving, and I realize the noise I heard wasn't entirely coming from him.

Pressing my ear against the wood, mentally apologizing for what feels like an invasion of privacy, I'm stunned when what sounds like my name reaches me. And while I'd find that flattering any other night coming from him, knowing he's dreaming of me as I was him earlier, his tone is currently filled with fear.

"Should we go check on him, Kevin?" I ask the dog, feeling guilty because he should be in there with Tank. If he was, maybe this wouldn't be happening. Kevin bumps the door with his nose. "I'll take that as a yes."

I don't make a peep as I let myself in, Kevin following me, but it doesn't matter as Tank is tossing and turning on the big bed, covers pooled around his waist. The woman in me takes a second – fine, three – to admire his bare chest, but I don't stop walking toward him at all.

He needs me. I don't know how or why I know that, but I do.

"Calliope!" I scream over and over. Praying for her to answer me, to find her, any outcome that will let me know she's okay. I know I'm dreaming even as I scour the town for her, but I don't stop. I can't. If I do, I'll lose her.

It's changed numerous times since meeting her, and this lets me know it's not done. Almost everything it used to be has faded and now starts and ends with Calliope. Thankfully, the part where I turned from her and discovered she was gone only happened once, but the things that replaced it are just as scary.

Something took her from me, but I don't know what or when, nor how I can stop it from occurring. For as surely as I'm falling for her, I know this is another warning despite the differences in how it unfolds.

I'm running forward, unable to see which direction I'm going, and I don't care. All I know is something is pulling me and I'm letting it, sure it's taking me to her. Calliope is that way, and if I don't get to her in time...

"Tank, I'm here. You found me." I roll toward her voice and reach out for the hand on my arm, urging her to the mattress where I instantly wrap my body around hers.

"Keep you safe."

"You will. You are. I'm not going anywhere."

"Promise?"

"Yes."

"Can't lose you." I'm still caught in the nightmare of it happening, my brain unable to function to the point where I can speak more than incomplete sentences, but it's enough for her to understand me. She kisses my cheek, my jaw, my lips, and finally, my heart, and it settles something inside me, allowing me to take a deep breath.

All is right in my world and I fall back to sleep, knowing as long as she's in my arms, she's safe. I'll destroy anything that tries to take her from me. There is no force on this earth that is more determined than a man is when it comes to protecting his future.

* * *

I wake with the scent of cinnamon and vanilla surrounding me, a unique smell I already associate with Calliope. Her hair is tickling my nose, but I force myself to ignore it, not wanting to risk waking her. I want to savor every second of this closeness.

For the first time since I started reliving that

night, I was able to go back to sleep, and I feel refreshed, as if my rest hadn't been disturbed at all. Thankful for the internal clock that means I haven't needed to set an alarm in years, I remain still until she begins to stir. "Morning," I greet her as she lifts her head to see me.

"Morning," she says with a smile. When she does this sexy little stretch, my right hand, which had been on her waist, drops. As it cradles her ass, my cock lengthens in my pajama pants at the tightness underneath my palm. Giving it a squeeze, I'm rewarded with a sound of pleasure I suddenly crave to have ringing in my ears. Her fingers skim my pecs, then move upward to cradle my cheek. "Sherman," she whispers, permission and need in her voice. "I'm ready. Are you?" In response, I use my grip to shift her so she's straddling me, and groan as her center comes in contact with my hardness.

"Fuck." This is my version of heaven, I think, only to discover I'm wrong when she slides up and down, and I realize I can feel her heat as my bottoms are thin and all she's wearing is a long shirt and panties. "We only go forward from here," I inform her.

"Wouldn't have it any other way." Flipping us so

I'm on top, I recline on my haunches and take in the visual she makes, knowing it's a sight I will never forget. She's breathtaking.

Pushing her shirt up, my dick jerks as her breasts are revealed, and she raises her arms, allowing me to lift it over her head. "I don't know where to start," I confess.

"How about right here?" She suggests, pointing at her mouth.

"Have I mentioned how much your brain turns me on?" Not that I let her answer. I'm too busy fusing my lips to hers, my fingers lowering to pinch her nipples. She gasps as I pull back, whether it's to protest the space I just put between us or because she likes what I'm doing to her, I'm not sure. However, as I flick one with my tongue before sucking on it, she urges me to do it harder. I do, then repeat the process on the other.

"Please," Calliope moans, raising her hips. Taking the hint, I shove her panties down, and she kicks them to the side, her legs wrapping around me afterward. While I'm distracted by that, she's determined to get me just as naked, and she's succeeding as the breeze from my slightly opened window hits the hair on my thighs. As I'm not wearing anything else but the pants, with that material no longer containing me, my cock falls on her, the head bumping her clit, both of us jerking at the sensation. My tip notches at her center, and I instinctively push forward, then force myself to stop.

"I'm clean," I inform her, the need to sink into her making my voice harsh. "It's been a helluva long time."

"Same for me on both, but I'm not on anything." Fuck. Not gonna lie, the idea of taking her bare makes me feel primal. That's okay, though. She and I are making a commitment right here, right now, so that'll happen. When I tell her any condoms I might have expired over a decade ago, she laughs, sending me deeper. And sealing both our fates.

"Muse, you can't do that shit." Of course, she does it again, then verbally tortures me.

"I'm good, cycle wise, and you can always pull out...if you want."

With a growl, I assure her, "I damn well *don't.*" I've never been irresponsible, and I'm not now. We were talking about signs earlier, and this is another, the possibility that making us one could make us three doesn't scare me. It seems right. If the warmth I feel coating my first few inches is any indication, she liked my response. Her heels dig into my ass, urging me on. I thrust forward until I can go no further, then throw my head back, throat working but no sound coming out. What I'm experiencing stole my ability to think, to breathe, to do anything but treasure this. And then I feel her walls flex around me, like she's resuscitating me, and I thread my fingers through hers, letting our joined hands support my weight as I rise up. Dragging myself from her is difficult, but I do it, leaving just the tip in, then I look down, and demand, "Watch us."

Our gazes drop, and we stare while I slowly merge our bodies, her whispered, "Sherman," causing me to lose all control as my pace becomes frantic. Somehow, with my lower half maintaining a speed I never knew I could move; my mouth cover hers, kissing Calliope as if punishing her for how fuckin' good she feels. Her hard nipples are scraping my chest, her breasts bouncing against it from the force of my drives, the lunges that are a staple of my workout giving my thighs some sort of superpower as they maintain this momentum. As her core tightens around me, the flutters begin, letting me know she's close, and it brings mine barreling forward. When we break apart, she says, "Together."

We tumble over simultaneously, and I reluctantly spill on her stomach, hating that it feels wasted. What if it would've taken, given us a son or daughter?

Dropping to the mattress, I roll and tuck her against me, my chest heaving from exertion as she asks, "Why?"

"I wanted to more than even I knew until just now, but didn't want us to have made that decision when our minds may not have been fully functioning."

"That makes sense." Her words say she understands, however, there's disappointment in her voice, and I wonder if she heard it in mine, too.

7

CALLIOPE

After we made love yesterday morning, Tank reluctantly went to work a couple hours later, with me assuring him multiple times I'd be okay on my own. And I was, even as part of me wished he'd been able to remain with me.

He'd offered to take me with him, and I'd contemplated it, but ultimately decided against it. Thirty minutes later, I was wishing I had gone. Which is what I did today.

Oh, I'd occupied myself, taking my meds eating up more time than I wish it did, then I'd relaxed for a bit, my usual routine after downing them, then played with Kevin. Not only have I begun falling for Tank, Kevin is stealing my heart, too. Thank goodness they're a package deal, a statement that made Tank laugh when I told him later when he'd called to check in.

Mo and Leo are nice guys, and obviously loyal to Tank, which I appreciate. They've made me laugh with some of their stories about Tank, and Mo even shared a few from when Tank was little as he's known him for so long.

My eyes have barely left Tank since we arrived. He's in his element here. Not that he wasn't when he was surrounded by his friends and fellow firefighters, but it's...more, I guess. He'd already admitted he feels closer to his dad when he's here, and I'm sure that has a lot to do with it, yet I get the idea that here, he's the man he would've been if the fire hadn't happened.

Our relationship, the speed with which we're moving, isn't for everyone, and it shouldn't be. He and I are the only two it concerns, and while it may have had a rocky start, I'd say we're on solid ground now.

"Calliope," is said in my ear, though I don't jump. I'd felt the charge in the air as he'd gotten closer, despite being lost in my thoughts. We're so attuned to each other already my body knows when he's near. I sound like a twit thinking such things, yet I'm sticking to it.

"Boss," I tease, shivering when his eyes heat at the title. Interesting.

"Naughty," he whispers as his hand slides up my thigh.

"Apparently, you bring it out in me."

"Good," Tank instantly responds. "You bored?"

"Honestly, no. I like watching you work."

"Grease and oil turns you on?"

"When it's covering you, yes." I'm barely done talking when he swoops in for a kiss, and my hands grip his arms as I hang on for dear life.

A throat clears, but Tank doesn't stop until he's finished, and even then, he eases back slowly, his gaze on mine the whole time.

"I needed that," he tells me.

"So did I," I admit.

"What's up, Leo?" He asks without looking away from me.

"Your two o'clock is here." Tank glances at his watch, then tells Leo he'll be there shortly since they're a bit early.

"I need to give my woman something first." Leo snickers, then walks away whistling, causing Tank to chuckle. I don't even comment on how he referred to me, I enjoyed it too much to question it. And that's exactly what I want to be. I'm starting to realize I can be Calliope, half of a whole, and Callie, a teacher. The latter I'm still debating if it's the correct choice for me, but the former? I yearn for it with every part of my being...as long as it's with the man in front of me. He takes my hand and helps me from the chair I'd been perched in, his own at his insistence. Given he has at least seven or eight inches on me, my feet didn't even skim the floor, so I'd been curled up in it.

"For a man that was a self-proclaimed loner, you sure did adapt to coupledom without any trouble," I point out.

"My dad told me he knew instantly that mom was meant to be his, as did his dad before him with my grandma. It may have scared me shortly after we met, but it wasn't because I doubted what you made me feel, only being able to survive without you."

We'd covered this when he'd gone to the B&B to apologize, yet I never asked the one thing I truly needed to know. "What made you change your mind?"

"Something Pops said." I wait, knowing this can't be rushed. "Even if I was only given a day with you, I knew it'd be one I would cherish forever, and regret it until my last breath if I walked away from what we could have." I don't feel the tears falling from my cheeks, though his thumbs brushing them off resonate through my soul. Rising to my tiptoes, his hands now cupping my face, I place a gentle kiss on his lips, hoping to convey how much he's coming to mean to me. I wish I could say or do more to let him know, but now isn't the time. And he knows it, too. "I want to take you into my office and ravish you," he warns me.

"And I'd let you."

"But I really do want to give you this." I open my mouth to be a smartass, but his expression is so earnest that I close it when I see what this means to him. He makes this sound deep in his throat, a mix of a growl and groan, then leads me through the bays and toward the back door we'd used this morning.

He covers my eyes the second it closes behind us, not even giving me a chance to look around. "This is obviously meant to be a surprise," I observe with a laugh.

Tank's free hand taps my ass, making my thighs clench, and it must not have been as subtle as I thought because I hear him muttering, "Just a few more hours."

"Could be minutes if we can sneak into that office of yours."

"No far using that beautiful voice you were named for to seduce me," he teases.

"Is it actually seducing when you want the same thing?" Deciding to have some fun, and not entirely joking, I continue with, "I can thank you prior to seeing my gift."

"How do you know you'll want to?" He asks, his tone suddenly serious.

"Because it's from you."

Tank

Once again, an answer that's complicated in its simplicity. Leading her forward, mindful of what's around us to ensure she doesn't hurt herself, I stop at our destination, second guessing what I'm about to do. When I remove my hand, she stares at the vehicle we're standing beside, then looks at me and returns to it.

"Do you like it?"

"It's beautiful," she tells me, and I know she truly means it.

Digging in my front pocket, the material tighter than it was now that it's trying to accommodate my eager dick, I pull out a keychain and inform her, "I'm glad you think so, since it's yours. If you want it."

"What? You...what?"

"You don't have a car here. Wait, do you even have one?" She nods, saying sort of, which means no in my book. "I'd gladly let you use my truck, but I need it in case I get called in. And when you get the job tomorrow," she's nervous about the interview, but I know they'll love her, "you'll need wheels to get there and home."

"Did a customer not pay their bill or something?" I laugh, telling her that's not how things work here. "I don't understand what's going on."

"After we, *I* fixed my fuck up, I made a few calls and was able to locate this. We both know you needed it, and my friend was eager to get rid of it. Not that there's anything wrong with it, he's a mechanic as well and I trust him completely, and that says a lot where your safety is concerned. It belonged to his mom, who didn't like to drive much, so it has low mileage and is in great condition."

"What do I owe for it?"

"Nothing." She starts to argue, but I refuse to budge on this. "It's my honor to do this for you. Please, let me."

"I feel as if I'm getting the better end of the deal."

"You'd be wrong. I now know you have reliable transportation, and can go somewhere if needed when I can't be with you." That last part must've revealed something I'd hoped to keep to myself because she apologizes, clearly reading between the lines.

"You hated me being alone yesterday, just in case."

"I prefer knowing you have transportation if you need it."

"Sherman," she calls me that when she wants me to pay attention, and when we're making love, and I've found I crave it from her lips, "I have good days and bad, but I know what triggers my allergies and asthma, and do everything in my power to avoid them."

"Could you tell me what they are, so I know, too?"

"Of course, though it might be easier to say what doesn't bother me." She's trying to ease the mood, and I appreciate that, but some things are serious, and her health is at the top of the list. Her smile fades, realizing I don't, *can't,* joke about this. Maybe I'll be able to in the future, but I'm not there yet. "I'll write them down, okay?" And I'll make sure I memorize them all.

Not wanting to ruin the day, or her joy at the new-to-her car, I tell her thank you, then ask if she'd like to take it for a spin. She nods, relief crossing her face that we weathered a conversation that could've easily turned tense. I hate that I can't go with her, but I promise she can drive me around later, stating it's her turn to chauffeur me now. Calliope giggles, and I know we're back on even ground again.

"Be careful, and call if you get lost."

"I have GPS," she reminds me with sass.

"You sure that'll work here?" I ask to mess with her. When she realizes it, she playfully smacks my arm, then acts as if she hurt it. I snatch it and kiss it, then do the same to her mouth, already missing her. "Got what you need?" She'd put a few items in a bookbag, time killers inside if she got bored, but her purse thingy is slung over her shoulder as it always is. Well, that's not true. It was the last thing on our minds when we fucked ourselves into exhaustion the past two nights as she never returned to the guest room, not that I'd let her, and her belongings are spread out among mine.

Surprisingly, I haven't had my nightmare aside from when she woke me from it. But I did get up with her around four this morning when she was having trouble breathing. I'd quickly grabbed her inhaler, shocked my hand wasn't shaking from the fear coursing through me, and watched intently as she used it, wanting to see how to operate it. When she blessedly experienced that first lungful of air trouble free afterward, I took in my own.

It's terrifying to see her like that, to know I really can't do anything but pray. I can only reassure myself she knows what she's doing and how to treat it, and the fact she doesn't panic helps calm my fears.

"I'm going to make you dinner as a thank you." Homecooked meal courtesy of her? Not turning that down.

"What about dessert?" I ask, curious how far I can go with this.

"That'll be me," she responds with a smirk, then gives me a quick kiss, reminds me to bring her bag home, and starts the car. She drives off, her hand tossing a wave at me from the open window, and I'm left standing there, wondering if I have time to jerk off. The visual of gorging on her later has my dick aching for release, which means there is currently no blood getting to my brain. Not a good idea when you work with machines of any kind.

Walking a bit awkwardly inside, I'm thankful my shirt is long enough to cover the evidence of what she does to me. I could take care of myself in the bathroom as I'd initially thought to just a few minutes ago, enabling the blood to rush back to my upper head so I can function, but it would leave me even more unsatisfied because she wasn't a part of it, it wasn't *us*. Now that I've met her, nothing will ever be the same without her.

Calliope

I still can't believe he bought me a car. It's the sweetest thing anyone has ever done for me, and I'm not saying that because of the cost, but the thought behind it is what's priceless.

Tank won't let me repay him with money for this, I already know that, so I will in other ways. One is the dinner I mentioned making for him, another is finishing the night making love.

At the store, I gather the ingredients I need, and pass the condom aisle on my way to the registers. We have some at the house as we purchased them after our first time together, though we don't always use them. Perhaps that's risky, and maybe too soon considering, but we agreed if we create a life, then we'll be ecstatic, and see it as another sign.

That might sound as if we're setting ourselves up for failure, or putting too much too soon on a new relationship, but we aren't teenagers with stars in our eyes, or in our twenties and just starting out. I'm not saying people can't find the one for them at those ages, simply that Tank and I are both established in our careers, well, I was in my previous field, and know what we want in a partner. Plus, the fact neither of us have been interested in dating for a long time until meeting is quite telling.

When I've paid and left the store, I place the groceries in the back seat, grinning as I close the door on my new car, and slide into the driver's seat. A few minutes after turning the key, I'm driving down the road, and I can't help but take in the scenery.

Landscape wise, the town is beautiful, idyllic even, but it's more than that. The residents care about each other, and I know a lot of that is because there are so few, but it doesn't lessen it.

This, this is what I was searching for as a kid. My parents are wonderful people that did the best they could for me and my brother. They also gave us a childhood I'm thankful for because it allowed me to experience different cultures. I learned so many things that can never be taught in a class-room and I cherish them all, but...yeah, I'm ready for this. The idea of walking into a building and more than likely knowing all the patrons in there makes me happy. Then again, maybe that cliché about the grass being greener has some truth to it because there are some that probably envy how I grew up and the life I had as a storm chaser.

I'd like my offspring to have the best of both worlds, a home they know will always be there and the chance to explore outside of it.

Once I get the bags in the kitchen, I put the food away as I don't need to start dinner yet all while Kevin dances at my heels hoping for a treat.

Deciding to relax for a bit, I make a cup of tea then head to the deck I was surprised to discover Tank and a few of his friends built. I can see us having cookouts here, enjoying a day with our family and friends, and I wonder if there will come a time that my parents choose to purchase a house and settle down. That sounds silly to think seeing as they're in their late fifties, but they've been wanderers since before they got married, and I'm not sure they'll ever be able to stop. Even if it'd be nice to have them close.

When I see a bee land on a flower, I instinctively pat my crossbody, despite already knowing my epi-pen is in there, and breathe a sigh of relief when it quickly moves on. It's not that I have anything against them, I know they have an important role, but they and numerous other species similar to them are potentially dangerous for me. Hell, yellow jackets are what started all this.

Which reminds me Tank wants to talk about that when he gets home. With my tea finished, Kevin and I go back inside and I locate a pen and notebook and write the list I promised. My test results were overwhelming at first, but I've learned it's better to face it head on, and find some humor in it when I can. I hope he can reach that level at some point, too.

With that task completed, I wash my hands then start dinner, and, as I'd hoped, I'm setting it on the table a couple minutes prior to Tank walking in the door.

He greets me with an enthusiastic kiss, one I'd love to take to the conclusion we're both craving, but I know he has to be hungry. The man can pack in the food.

I ask about the rest of his shift as I'd left before lunch, and he answers my questions. I know nothing about cars, but I'm happy to listen to him discuss them, just as he does when I share things that interest me.

He falls silent after thanking me a second time for cooking, and saying how good it is, then breaks it by initiating our discussion. "How'd you discover your allergies? There's usually something that leads to getting tested for them, right?"

"Ironically, from jogging."

Tank laughs, saying, "That's supposed to make people healthier, sweetheart."

"Well, I like to be different," I respond with a smile. "I had a usual route I followed, even though it's recommended you not do that," I add the last bit when he frowns at me. "However, I did switch it up by turning left instead of right, and that was a big mistake that day. I'm still not exactly sure how it happened, but I think I accidentally kicked a rock and it hit a nest of yellow jackets. Understandably, they didn't take too kindly to that and saw me as a threat."

"Oh shit," he almost growls, probably visualizing what that meant.

"Yeah. I didn't know what was going on at first, just felt a pinch, then another, and a third, and so on. I was finally able to get away, but I'd already been stung over ten times from the thighs down to my ankles. The pain hit instantly, shooting through both legs, and I'm not ashamed to admit I was bawling because it was so excruciating."

"They inject a poisonous venom, and with so many of them..." His expression of horror tells me he's imagining it, and I don't have the heart to tell him it's more than likely even worse than that. I never want to experience that level again in my life.

"It didn't take long before the areas around each turned red, then started to swell. Later, I realized it was not only because of the amount of it overwhelming my system, but I'm highly allergic to them. On a positive note," I state only for him to scoff.

"There *is* one?"

"Took me a while to find it, but yes. If that hadn't occurred, who knows how long I would've gone undiagnosed."

"I love that you were able to find something good about this, it's a testament to your character, to how you were raised."

"Eh, if that were the case, I would've told my family right away."

"Cut yourself some slack," he urges me. "It's a lot to deal with."

"And I've had to do it alone because I didn't tell them."

"Could they have done anything if you had?"

"You mean, besides give me comfort and support? Maybe visited and held my hand during the testing?"

"Okay, fine. You're a horrible daughter and sister. Is that what you wanted to hear? Does it change the past?" I raise a brow at that, he and I knowing there's still some lingering blame about his dad. "Yeah, I heard it," he confesses, "and I'm working on it." I simply nod, knowing that's all he can do. I can't force Tank to forgive himself. "Back to you," he leads off, and I let him deflect. For now.

"They took blood, and I learned some of my issues, but they recommended the skin testing as well. When they did the first round on my arm, my reaction was immediate. Almost forgot, about a week and a half after the incident," I smirk at my term for it, "I was bit by two mosquitoes on my right arm." Not a big deal, usually, unless you're me. "About twenty minutes later, I had hives over the entire upper portion of my body. Wrists to shoulders, chest, neck, back. I was miserable."

"Which means we need to be careful with you when they're out, or could be. Especially when it's been raining."

"Ready to run screaming for the hills yet?"

"Never," he informs me with no hesitation, confident in himself, in us. I knew in my heart that would be his response, but hearing it settles that last bit of fear I'd been harboring. I send him a grateful smile, then continue my story.

"So, when they saw how quickly it impacted me, and that's with the stuff to help limit the allergic reaction, they decided to do more."

"How many more exactly?" He asks, grimacing.

"In total, just a couple shy of a hundred." That's

when I slide the list toward him, his mouth dropping open in shock as he scans it. "I warned you the non-allergies would be easier."

"Nature is trying to kill you," he jokes, making me laugh. I know then he'll eventually be able to laugh with me about this. I've found it actually helps, as weird as that sounds.

"That's what I told the doctor," I admit.

"Bees, paper bees – that's a thing? – wasps..." he reads. "Grass, trees, dust, ragweed."

"Oh no," I interrupt him, "not just ragweed, but *all* of it. Your girl is an overachiever. And, because of that particular one, I have to be mindful of other stuff."

"Such as?" He asks, sincerely interested. Tank's hand, a pen from his shirt pocket now in it, is poised above the paper, ready to take notes.

"Chamomile, for instance, is a relative of it and can bother me."

"And you have to be even more careful because of your asthma. Breathe in too much of something you shouldn't..." Yeah, it could be really bad. "With your visible reactions, how'd you hide it from your friends?"

"It was summer, so flowy dresses and skirts were my friend as they were long enough to cover to my ankles. As for shoes, it was painful to wear them, so when I couldn't go barefoot, I wore flip flops as they were the loosest. But I still kicked them off as soon as I could." During the worst of it, they blamed it on me coming down with something, which wasn't too far from the truth as I was pretty stationary during the worst of it. I tried so many home remedies, vinegar being one of them. It wasn't pleasant, but it worked.

He quietly stands, shoves his feet back into his boots, grabs a trash bag from under the kitchen sink, and goes onto the deck.

"Whatcha doin'?"

"These flowers and plants have to go." Then he starts scooping them up, prepared to get rid of all of them because they can pose a threat to me. Putting me first.

He saw potential danger where I'm concerned and didn't hesitate to act on solving it. If that isn't a testament to the kind of man he is, I don't know what is.

8

CALLIOPE

The interview went well. Okay, I nailed it, and that's not just confidence talking. I have evidence to back it up. During the first round, we discussed my background, in addition to why I was thinking of retiring from storm chasing to begin using my teaching degree.

I was completely honest, something I know I need to start being with my family and friends, and told Mr. Jackson about my asthma and allergy issues. He was very sympathetic, understanding why it would make me question my future with the team. He was also enthusiastic about what my knowledge of the weather could bring to the staff.

When he asked if I'd be interested in meeting the board, I eagerly said yes, of course, not realizing he meant then. I discovered they were the second and final round, and before I knew it, they were going over the salary, benefits, and wondering if I could start next week. I was too shocked to do anything but nod, and walked around in a daze as they gave me a tour of the school and showed me the classroom that would be mine.

The whole time, all I wanted to do was call Tank and tell him the good news, but I resisted, deciding to do it in person instead. Which is what I'm on my way to do. I'm running a lot later than expected since I hadn't planned on being there for three hours, but it was worth it.

My face hurts from smiling so much, something I thought would make others look at me strangely, but they merely return it with a friendly wave. Pulling into the driveway, I brush my hand along the dashboard of my car, loving the sedan Tank was thoughtful enough to find for me. I don't see his truck yet, and I'm shocked I beat him home.

As I open my door, I laugh when Kevin immediately jumps over me and into the passenger seat. "Sweetheart, we'll go for a ride later, okay? Why are you outside?"

That question is answered when a woman's

voice states, "That would be my doing." Ummmm… When I look up, I see Tank's sister, recognizing her from when he'd pointed her out at the fair, and various pictures around the place. This is my first time actually meeting her.

"Hello, Bree. I'm Callie." Since Tank started using my full name, I've discovered that I don't like introducing myself as such, keeping those that address me as Calliope a select bunch that means the world to me. Not that my friends don't, it's just…different. "Tank didn't mention you were coming over." I hope that didn't sound as defensive as it did in my ears.

Thankfully, she grins, letting me know, "I like to stop by randomly, just to throw him off. But as it seems you're living here now, I, uh, think I'll quit doing that." When she laughs, a potentially awkward situation is diffused, and I'm relieved.

"He shouldn't be much longer," I offer. "You're welcome to stay and wait for him." I grab my bag from the passenger side floor, then check my phone as Kevin proceeds to exit his spot, reluctantly. I'm about to text Tank to let him know she's here as I didn't have one from him, only to see my screen light up with him calling me. "Sorry I didn't you call you after the interview, but I just got home," I tell Tank as I know he was as excited about it as me.

"Say that again," he urges. I repeat it, though I'm unsure why since I don't hear a lot of noise in his background. "No, not all of it. The last part." What? Oh.

"Home." The groan that travels through the speaker is reminiscent of the one he makes during orgasm, and I'm suddenly aware of the fact I'm standing outside, my boyfriend's sister in front of me, and all I can think about is the ache growing between my legs. "Speaking of," I interrupt as I casually turn around in hopes of muffling my voice, "when will you be here? I'm feeling lonely now. Plus, we need to celebrate."

The noise following that is not a happy one. "Fuck, muse. I'd be there and inside you in five minutes if I could. I forgot we had a quick meeting tonight."

"Oh," I respond, as disappointed as he is. "That's okay."

"I'll be there as soon as I can. You gonna be in my favorite lingerie?"

"You're such a goof," I tease, knowing full well he's referring to one of his shirts.

"What? You are sexy as fuck in my clothes."

"Even better without them," I taunt, smirking when he mutters about me making it difficult for him to walk. "Drive safe," I add, picturing him getting pulled over for speeding in a hurry to get here. He says he won't dare risk getting to me any later than he already is, then we hang up when the meeting is about to start.

"So," Bree singsongs when I'm facing her again, "you two sound close."

"Am I blushing as much as I think I am?"

She inspects my cheeks, then states, "Probably more."

When Tank joins us almost two hours later, she and I are in the living room laughing, a bond forming that may have started due to our respective relationships to Tank but will grow because of her and I. He makes a beeline for me, gives me a toe-curling kiss, then ruffles Bree's hair, which makes her glare at him.

"I'm twenty-five," she tells him.

"Not yet," he corrects her.

"Close enough."

"Don't rush it." Then he glances at me, and indicates her with a tip of his heads. "Kids these days, amirite?"

"Don't quit your day job," Bree chimes in as she

rolls her eyes, but she's smiling, the affection between them clear to see. I'm looking forward to meeting Carly as well and seeing all three of them together. It also makes me miss Slade. It's been at least a year since I saw him, which isn't rare due to our schedules, but talking on the phone regularly isn't the same as being able to hug him. "Besides," I tune back in as she continues razzing him, "everyone is a kid compared to you."

"You saying I'm an old man?"

"If the gray hair fits…"

"Who do you think put it there?" He quips.

"Carly," she responds without hesitation.

Seeing this could go on for a while, I get involved. Not to stop it, but to play along. "Talk a little louder, Bree, he didn't put his hearing aid in today." She raises her hand toward me for a high-five, which I gleefully give, making Tank mutter about us ganging up on him.

"You're just jealous your girlfriend is on my side."

"I can take you, pipsqueak."

"Oh yeah? I'll tell Mom." Then she laughs when Tank shudders, wiping pretend tears from her eyes. "Scared of her, aren't you?"

"Any sane person would be. That woman could

make a drill sergeant cry if he pissed her off." Then Tank grins at me, as if in comfort, and says, "Don't worry, she'll adore you. Now, share your good news. I know you got the job," he demands, apparently no longer able to wait.

"I did," I state, then tell them about the interviews. Tank picks me up and swings me around, then plants a passionate kiss on me.

"It's another sign this is where you're meant to be," he whispers, staring directly into my eyes then placing a sweet kiss on my forehead.

"That's what I think, too," I admit.

"Would you be okay meeting my mom? If you aren't ready, I understand." This obviously means a lot to him, and I get that as I want him to meet my family, too. It's a testament to how serious we are.

"Psst…Bree." When she turns to me, I ask, "What can she be bribed with?"

At my question, Tank moves to my side, his arm now around my waist, and I catch the siblings glance at each other before simultaneously answering, "Grandbabies."

Tank

Conversation continued after that, but my mind remained on what I'd said. I've never really thought about having kids, the loss of my dad something I didn't want to risk my own experiencing. And it was a possibility since there are dangers involved with firefighting, even in the small towns we cover. Yet having them with Calliope? I suddenly want a house full of them.

"Tank," Bree calls, getting my attention, "we boring you?" Then she mock whispers to Calliope, "He doesn't like to read."

"I do, too." She arches a brow – dang it, I wish I could do that – until I concede. "Fine. I really don't." She shakes her head as she tsks, lamenting the fact we're related.

"Did you know," Calliope starts, and I can't wait to hear what random information she knows on books. I've started to live for these little drops of how she thinks, how her brain works. "The earliest things written were more than likely administrative lists, and that was on clay tablets." Bree looks a bit shocked, but I want to know more.

"What's the oldest book?"

"It's reported to be The Epic of Gilgamesh, an accounting, mythologically speaking, of his rule." Bree never one to miss an opportunity to tease, returns to the earlier joke about my age.

"Didn't you two go to school together?"

"I think Mom is calling you."

She scoffs, then eagerly turns back to her book bestie, as she's now referring to her, with an, "Anyway," and begins talking about an author's last release. "The way he weaves together a story is a gift. It always keeps me guessing who the bad guy is and what they'll do next."

"Those are the best kind," Calliope agrees, to which Bree nods. "Who is it?"

"I know this one," I interrupt, raising a hand, telling her with a wink I'm getting her prepared for the students on Monday.

"Yes, Sherman?" She quips, and fuck if that teacher voice doesn't turn me on. If she had glasses and slid them down to the edge of her nose before she'd said that my head might explode…both of them.

Calliope drinks some of her water as I reply, "Lawrence Slater." When she chokes, I quickly pat her back, carefully watching to make sure she's okay.

She flashes me a thumbs up, knowing I was worried, and informs me it went down the wrong pipe. "You really like his stuff, huh?" She asks Bree who nods.

"He's quite talented."

"That he is." I'm not sure why Calliope is smiling, unless she's a fan of his, too, and it sounds as if she is. And that makes me jealous. "Do you have all his books?"

"Only the digital versions."

"Hmm..." There's that grin again. What is she up to?

* * *

"I told you that you'd get the job," I remind her after my sister leaves, the two of them hugging as if they're the best of friends.

"Yes, you did. How did you know?"

"They'd be stupid not to hire you."

"You're a little biased where I'm concerned."

"A lot," I amend. "Plus, you're meant to be here." I shrug, figuring that says it all. She creeps closer, fingers pulling her shirt up and over her head. I stay quiet, not wanting to interrupt. She shimmies her shorts down her lean thighs and lets them fall at her bare feet, then steps out of them and continues moving toward me. "Am I about to get schooled, Ms. Lawrence?"

The answer is yes, because she brings me to my knees, after she drops to hers.

9

TANK

May…

The past couple weeks have been hectic as Calliope adjusts to her new position, though she's loving every minute of it. I also discovered the storm team's videos and watched any I could find, fast forwarding until she was on screen. It's easy to see she was proud of what they were doing, but I could see the change occurring in her eyes. She was ready for the next phase, even if she didn't know it at the time.

Currently, she's relaxing on the bed while I'm sitting on the floor leaning against it, listening to her tell a story about one of her students as I pet

Kevin. "I'd told the kids the other day how you can teach a dog to count."

"What now?" I ask in shock.

"All you need is patience and their attention focused on you. Then you use commands, for example, 'tell me,' and 'say one.' Eventually, they'll begin barking the correct number of times as requested."

"So, they just remember the sequence," I state, assuming I have it all figured out.

"But what if you always mix it up? No two "lessons" are the same."

"Can we teach Kevin?" Kevin perks his head up, knowing his name. Then she blows my mind by showing me as he counts up to ten.

She shrugs, admitting, "I wanted to work with him to make sure it was possible first." I'm staring at Kevin, telling him how good a boy he is, praising him for being so smart.

"What did he do?" I ask, getting back to her story.

Calliope giggles, saying, "I went to collect their homework, and when I got to Stevie's desk, he looked right at me, and with a straight face informed me that his dog ate it."

"That old excuse? Kids can't come up with anything better nowadays?"

"It's an oldie but goodie," she informs me, "and he did put his own twist on it. When I asked why, he calmly told me that he fed it to Bowser."

"Wait? He admitted that he did it on purpose?"

"Yep, but he wasn't done. I again wanted to know why." I'm so into this, needing to know what he said, I quickly ask what his response was. "He didn't have time to teach him how to count the way I talked about, so he took a shortcut."

It takes me a minute to realize what he meant, and when I do, I throw my head back and laugh until I'm close to crying. "He believed his dog would learn instead by eating his math homework?" Turning to look at her, she nods, eyes twinkling, happiness radiating from her. I believe there are moments that become embedded in your heart, memories you never lose, and this is one of mine.

Right here. Right now. This is when I fell in love.

Calliope

Seeing Tank as amused by Stevie as I was sticks with me for hours. We could've easily stayed home and enjoyed some time to ourselves, but it was Sunday, and his mom invited us over for dinner. It would just be the three of us, probably Tank's doing, so I wouldn't be overwhelmed, even though I assured him that his sisters could've come. Bree and I get along great, and I'm sure Carly and I will, too.

When we walked in, his mom had hollered from the kitchen to let us know where she was, and Tank had taken my hand, silently reminding me he had me, then led the way. I know this isn't the house he'd grown up in, and my heart still aches for their loss, of Otto and the memories they'd made within those four walls, but I can tell they brought him here with them, images of a man they've never forgotten spread throughout the house.

There are pictures of the five of them on the mantle, of Tank and a man that looks a lot like Tank does now, and so many others. It's a tribute to how much they love, for it's definitely not past tense, him.

"Aren't you gorgeous?" I hear as we round a corner. I blush and start to tell her thank you, but

Tank's smartass switch has apparently been flipped.

"Mo-om," he responds, dragging it out, "you know I prefer the phrase 'handsome as all get out.'" She smacks his arm with a dish towel, to which he grabs his elbow and jumps around as if it actually hurt. I gotta tell ya, a man his size doing that is a sight to see. She shushes him, not in the least surprised by his antics, then stands in front of me, shifting from side to side as she hops on one foot then the other. "She wants to hug you," he informs me. "She's big on that, and if you don't let her know she can in the next two seconds, she might burst from her skin with anticipation." I assume he's teasing, but when I smile at her, she engulfs me, and swings us to the right then left, like she's rocking me. It's the sweetest thing.

"Sherman," I begin, feeling her jerk against me when I call him that, "I'm stealing your mom, okay? You've had her for almost forty years, so I think it's time you share her with others. And by others, I mean me. Mrs. Reardon," she instantly corrects me, "sorry, Lorna," she pats my cheek in approval after that, "can I bribe you to..."

"No need, dear," she interrupts me, "once you and Tank are married, you'll be my kid, too. Shoot, let's just go ahead and say you are now, no since waiting. I know my boy, and he'll be poppin' the question before long." What now? I sneak a peek at Tank and find him smiling, not in the least bothered by his mom's declaration. As we help her put the food on plates and in bowls, she continues to her next target. "And now Carly has a new man in her life," Tank mentioned that, as well as his concerns because of her ex, Eric, or as Tank called him, fuckstick. "Soon, my babies will have babies. Just need to find a guy that deserves Bree, and all of my children will be happy. If only your dad was here. He'd be tickled pink."

Tank glances at me, has the nerve to blow me a kiss, and the only thing he comments on is, "Rick," she corrects him that it's Ross, which he knows and grins at with a wave of his hand and a, "whatever," such a child sometimes, "has been warned."

"He's not dickhead," Lorna reminds him, making me crack up. "What?" She asks me. "That's what he is. Be thankful I didn't use the nickname everyone else does for him." She has a point. I have a few of my own for him after what he did, or tried to do, to us. The only reason he's still alive is we weren't in the living room when the shot was fired through the window. Tank and I were in bed with

Kevin snoring on his own. We can't prove it was Eric, but the fact Tank had an eye-opening chat with the corrupt sheriff, Eric's buddy, prior to it is not a coincidence. And Tank didn't hesitate to let the sheriff know he isn't the only one aware of what he's been up to.

The rest of our dinner is about more pleasant topics, her job, mine, etc. When it's time to leave, I feel we've made a good start in getting to know each other, and confident that she approves of me for her son. Not that it's necessary, he's a grown man after all, but it makes things easier in the long run.

She gives me a hug before we leave, thanking me. When I ask why, she says for loving her son. And she's right, I do. I've been falling every day since meeting him, but I knew I was gone for him when Lorna started mentioning marriage, and I *saw* us standing in front of an altar. I heard us saying our vows.

I want that future for us more than my next breath.

10

CALLIOPE

Sitting at my desk during lunch, I decide to call Slade for a couple reasons. One, it's been a while since we talked, and two, I need a favor.

After we catch up for a few minutes, he surprises me. "I'm coming to visit next month."

"Really?"

"I told you I'd be doing so soon the last time we chatted, so why do you sound shocked?" Good question. I honestly don't know why. It isn't rare; it just doesn't get to happen often.

"No idea," I admit. "Just caught me off guard, I guess."

"What's going on?" Not quite ready to jump into the news that'll get his big brotherness, it's a thing, in high gear, I decide to ease into it.

"Umm, I'm not at home. Well, actually, I am, but not the one you think."

"That makes so much sense," he jokes.

"It started when Jemma invited me to her hometown."

"Which isn't unusual. You two have been close for years."

"True, but this was for a special reason." Then I tell him about the ceremony and the reason for it, mentioning the guys individually instead of as a whole.

"Is this Tank," he huffs as he says the name, causing me to shush him, "the reason you're still in Trapley?"

"I see what you did there, both times," I admonish him. "Cut it out." He acts innocent, but I'm not buying it. "Also, how did you know?"

"Your voice got all sickly sweet when you said it." He gives a fake shudder, the exaggerated sound he adds for added impact letting me know what he's doing. Butthead.

"You ever gonna grow up?"

He laughs, then says, "You first."

"So, that's a no. And yes, he's part of it, but I've been thinking about a change for a while. This trip just helped me take those final steps."

"There's more you aren't telling me." He's not wrong, though I am for continuing to keep it from him and our parents.

"Anyway," I reply, avoiding that sticky situation yet again, "can you send me a signed copy of each of your books?"

"You already have them," he reminds me, which is true. He always sends me an autographed version of every title, and I cherish them. Which leads to me making a mental note that I need to return to Austin to grab them as well as my other stuff.

"These are for Tank's youngest sister. She's a fan and her birthday is next month. "

"And my work is your way of punishing her?"

"You're a pain in my ass, you know that?"

"I do, and I'm very good at it." I don't deny that.

"Yes, I thought she'd appreciate them, for some reason. Besides, she's probably your only fan other than family," I tease. But when I hear him mutter what sounds like he wishes, I realize he has his own secrets. Which I can't very well call him out on right now unless I'm ready to spill mine. Thwarted by my own hesitation. Cowardice. They both apply.

"Of course, you know all you have to do is ask." I also know he won't let me pay for them, he never does for anything, so I'll have to be sneaky. Perhaps another donation to his favorite charity? He doesn't know I've been doing it, which is the whole point, and it allows me to feel better, as if I'm not doing all the taking and him the giving. It's silly, but there you go.

When the bell rings signaling my break is over, we say bye, then I gather my stuff and throw away the trash. Today we're discussing science, more specifically the weather, and, once they find out my previous job was chasing storms, their hands don't stop going up and down for the next hour.

"Do you get speeding tickets while you're doing it?"

"How many pairs of shoes do you go through?" That from a kid who thought I literally ran after them.

"Did you get caught in one before?"

"Do you have to live in your car?"

"Do you miss Christmas?"

"Why are you here? Did you get in trouble?"

"Is it gonna rain tomorrow?"

"Do you have to call your parents a lot?" This

question stays with me after they've left for the day and I'm driving toward mine.

Using the hands-free feature, I activate my cell and ask it to dial mom, knowing she'll put it on speaker, allowing dad to speak to me, too.

"Calliope!" She exclaims. "We were just talking about you."

"I didn't do it. Slade did." Dad laughs, Mom tsks, and I defend myself by questioningly offering, "Reflex?"

Dad reminds Mom, "Our son would do the exact same thing."

"He would," I chime in.

"The both of you are so alike," Mom states. "Now, tell us why you sound so happy."

"Did I not before?" I ask. "Slade wanted to know that as well."

"Honey, it's not that you seemed miserable, just…"

Dad finishes for Mom, the two of them always in sync, "we knew you were struggling."

"I was," I admit.

"But not any longer?"

"Well, I'll answer that with something that will make you happy. Okay, maybe relieved is a better word." Mom starts crying, and I hear Dad sniffling a bit, those reactions a testament to how much they worry about me, and kept it to themselves. It's times like this I know how lucky I am to have them. They put aside their fears because they are firm believers in everyone following their own path, not that it means they won't celebrate if we take a different, less dangerous one. For example, the party they threw, giving any villager they saw, a piece of cake when Slade left the service. Yes, he was injured, but it could've been so much worse. I have a feeling they'll be baking a few dozen as soon as we hang up.

I repeat the story I shared with my brother, both eagerly asking about my students, what I'm teaching them, have they offered me the position permanently yet. I answer them, but have to correct them when they assume I'm staying with Jemma while I look for a place.

"Are you going to rent or buy?" Mom wants to know. When I tell her neither, she's confused, not understanding what I mean, until I explain that I met someone. Wincing at the shriek that brings on, I brace myself as the real grilling begins.

They request – it's an order – that I send a

picture of the two of us, and to call back soon when he's with me, as they want to interrogate, err get to know him. I promise to do both, tell them I love them, then hurry inside after parking in our driveway to warn Tank.

11

TANK

"Where is she?" I yell to the universe, fear clogging my throat so badly the words are almost inaudible. What if she needs me? I promised to take care of her, that I'd protect her from everything, but I can't do that if, "I can't fucking find her!"

"Sherman," I hear over and over, and finally realize it's Calliope, whispering my name in my ear like a mantra, her hand gentle yet firm on my arm. And I somehow know she doesn't want to risk yanking me out of my nightmare, the theory being you should ease people back to reality, instead. I appreciate the thoughtfulness, but I'd much rather the other in this case.

I grab her, pulling her against me as if to merge us, hating the space between us, as miniscule as it is right now, as if even that little bit will make my terror of losing her come true. "You're here," I state, my brain still locked in the world where she'd been taken from me. "I need you," I tell her.

"Then take me," she agrees, aware the closeness will soothe the beast roaring inside me, the terror of losing her like a living, breathing demon threatening to steal my sanity. I kiss her, mentally apologizing that her lips might be bruised from the force of it, but she eagerly returns it. Without breaking contact, thankful we chose to forego clothing before going to bed, I caress every inch I can on my way to her pussy, my touch rougher than usual, but again, she's enjoying it. At least her moans say she is, so does the cream coating my fingers as I reach my destination.

"You know, muse, I'm starting to feel inspired," then I retrace the path my fingers had just taken with my tongue, my lips, my teeth. "Tomorrow, you'll see my bite on your body as you get ready for work, feel it throughout your day while you're trying to concentrate on the lesson. What do you think of that? Does the idea of seeing my marks turn you on?" I ask as I begin to nibble on her clit. "Will you wear them with pride?"

"Like a badge of honor," she replies breathlessly,

and that answer is exactly what I wanted to hear. There's no finesse as I dive in, no method to how I eat her. I simply devour her, needing her to come, to taste her and know she's okay and nothing will take her from me. I will fight anything that tries. Fate itself won't defeat me. She's mine.

Two orgasms later, her juices dripping down my throat and covering my chin, I crawl up, and kiss her again, her moan as our combined scents hit her taste buds spurring me on.

"Put me in," I demand. "Take me in your hand and show me where you want me." She does so, the slight tremor in her grip almost my undoing as it lets me know she needs this just as I do. As her walls begin to surround me, she clenches, making veins pop out on my forehead as I push through, the resistance making her even tighter. "Fuck!" I holler, then slam inside, her shout of pleasure equaling mine. It's hard and fast, and just the beginning of what we do to each other the rest of the night. We'll both be dragging come morning, but I'll be smiling the whole damn time, when I'm not yawning or pounding back the coffee that is. Before we close our eyes, an hour prior to her alarm going off, I lay my hand over her heart, hers resting on mine, and tell her what

I've kept inside for too long. "I love you, Calliope."

And when she responds, "I love you, Sherman." This time when I dream, it's of me on my right knee, the ring I bought weeks ago in my hand, and asking her to be my wife. I don't know it, but I smile in my sleep as she accepts. I slide it on, then listen with rapt fascination as she tells me what the first ones were made of and why they're on the left ring finger.

12

CALLIOPE

June…

Tank has woken up every night the past few weeks, my voice and touch the only thing that can calm him. He's not eating, he's barely sleeping, and it's taking a toll on him. I wish I knew what to do to make it stop.

He's told me what his dreams have meant in the past, but the fact that they've changed, no longer including his dad at all, is very telling. Of what, I have no clue, and I worry that if we don't figure it out soon, it'll slowly drive him crazy because he can't continue to function this way. As if he isn't already on edge, this season means my allergies are in high gear, and he is hyperaware of them. He wasn't kidding when he said he'd memorize them. He knows what they all are and steers me from them if necessary.

Of course, I can't avoid them completely, and he knows this, but he's so sweet to try. Tank isn't obnoxious about it, but he does it so covertly I don't even realize it until later. It could be something as simple as taking my hand and veering another direction, or replanting the flowers farther from the deck, so there's less chance of me getting stung. If I didn't already love him…If I didn't already know he loves me…

There's only a week left of class, and it makes me sad. I'm going to miss the kids. I was a bundle of nerves leading up to my first day, but the second I'd stood in front of the room and introduced myself; they'd evaporated.

I was where I was meant to be, and the school appeared to agree as they'd offered me the position permanently. I'd accepted immediately, resisting the urge to hug them for asking. Tank was just as happy, and we'd celebrated for hours, and it wasn't all in bed. Part of it had been planning a trip to Austin to pack my things and bring them to his, *our*, house. He was so anxious to get it done he wanted to leave right after the final bell rang for the summer. His pout when I told him we couldn't was adorable.

It's not that I didn't want to, I was just as eager as he was, but there was really no rush as I had everything I needed here. Aside from a few cherished items, the rest can honestly wait, though I have a feeling Tank will keep urging me to do it sooner rather than later.

The kids are too excited to really pay attention, not that there's much going on. The teachers planned it so our lessons are already done, and testing is almost completed, which means we've spent today's class sharing our summer plans.

"We're gonna visit my grandpa and grandma," Brayden enthusiastically announces. "My dad said grandma's a lot, so he's packing earplugs." I quickly turn my head to hide my laughter, but I don't think I made it in time. The others giggle, and Brayden smiles proudly at being funny.

"I'm getting a dog," Ashley tells us, making her classmates jealous. The next hour entails questions on what kind, what games she'll play with it, boy or girl, what she'll name it, and if they can come over when she gets it. That leads to Leslie suggesting Ashley have a party so they can all meet her new puppy.

Stevie tells her to start teaching her new pet soon, as in feeding it homework. He swears it worked on Bowser. His mom admitted he asked to bring him to school to prove it, even pointing out that I like dogs, which I do, but she stood her ground. Of course, my money is on him, and on the final day, he begs us to walk outside with him, where Bowser is waiting in the car with Stevie's mom, and the dog obediently "counts" to five before the other kids have to go.

13

CALLIOPE

I caved, but in my defense, Tank can be very persuasive.

School has ended, making me free for the summer, at least until I get bored and find something else to do until it starts again. I was sad on the last day, as well as excited. Not as much as the kids were, of course, but I'm looking forward to having this time with Tank and getting to explore my new town more.

And yes, in case that wasn't already clear to everybody, this is now home. It's where I belong. Tank, however, wants to make it as official as possible, which is why we're currently loading the truck with a few things for our drive to Austin.

Tank was worried there wouldn't be enough

space to load my belongings, despite my reassurance I didn't have a lot, something I'm still trying to convince him of.

"Sherman," I say, knowing it's the easiest way to get his attention, aside from me getting naked. That's proven quite effective.

"Yes, my love," he drawls, emphasizing his accent as he knows it drives me wild. As if he isn't already a dangerous package. He smirks when he hears me sigh, the smug jerk.

I throw my hands over my ears, then begin chanting, "La la la la la." It doesn't work, not that I thought it would. Plus, I feel his laughter as he pulls me against him. "You don't play fair."

"Nope."

"And you aren't even sorry about it."

"Nope," he repeats as he picks me up, my feet dangling, and drops a kiss on my nose.

"You think you're so cute, that you can just smile and get your way."

"Do you think I'm cute?" I do. "That's all that matters." Yeah, that makes me wanna swoon, and jump his bones at the same time.

"Nope," I use his seemingly new favorite phrase, giggling when he frowns and looks at me with sad eyes, giving me a glimpse of how he probably tried to get out of trouble when he was little. "Somehow I don't see that working on your mom." He laughs and admits it didn't.

"She caught on pretty quickly, but it was worth a try today."

"Are you saying I'm an easy mark? A softie?"

"You love me, so...yes?" Good answer.

Wrapping my legs around his waist, I confess, "This is true. And you love me." His answer isn't verbal, but he's proven that he's more a man of action than words, that he's great at those, too, since the beginning, so it makes sense.

My back hits the vehicle just as his mouth takes mine. The different sensations are intoxicating, a complete contradiction of hard and soft, yet it fits Tank perfectly.

* * *

An hour later than we'd planned, we're on the road, and I am not complaining. It was worth it. We'd decided to bring Kevin with us, and we compromised by borrowing a trailer instead of renting a moving truck. Tank had pointed out I might want to load some of my bigger items after all. He could be right, so it's nice to have the option.

The drive is a little more than two hours each way, yet we'd chosen to make it an overnight trip. I'm not sure if we'll stay in my room or look for a pet friendly hotel, but we have time to figure that out.

After hitting a drive-thru for breakfast, we agree to take the scenic route, neither in a hurry as we're off the next two days. Tank has Mo and Leo covering for him, and Pops assured him they'd be fine without him. His wording might've been a bit more colorful, though.

We make stops as we head to Austin, bathroom breaks for us and Kevin, as well as to do some sightseeing. I've lived in this state for years, but you never really take the time to enjoy what you have in your own backyard, so to speak.

"Nice house," Tank comments when we pull into the drive. Whereas I felt more at peace the closer we'd gotten to Tarpley when Brittney, the team, and myself had made the drive a couple months ago, the reverse is true now. Oh, not in regards to me, but Tank. I know this part of my life is done, and I'm good with that, but his fingers have been tapping on his leg for the past twenty minutes. The beat has not been a pleasant one either.

"Your SOS has been received," I say softly, placing my hand on his.

He turns to glance at me, opens his mouth, then closes it. He takes a deep breath then offers, "Sorry. It's just…it looks like a good place to live."

"It is," I tell him, "and will continue to be so for the others. But I happen to prefer my *home* back in Tarpley now."

"You sure you won't miss this?"

"My friends, yes, but we can visit and talk on the phone. The constant traveling? No."

"And the rush that comes from what you do, did?" He corrects himself.

"That can be garnered in various ways."

"It won't be the same."

"True," I concede, "but that doesn't make it any less exciting."

"I beg to differ," I respond. "The things I'm talking about are even more so." He watches me, his eyes never leaving my face as I lean forward and kiss him. "There's an example. What we did this morning is another. Planning our future is a third. Having a new batch of students in the fall a fourth."

His smile is so bright, so hopeful, that it's almost blinding in its beauty, which might be weird to use in regards to a man, but there's really no other way to describe it. He looks so happy, and the knowledge that it's because of me is a feeling like nothing I've ever experienced. Even if I did have doubts, which I don't, about leaving this part of my life behind, this moment would've shown me this is the correct decision.

"Have you told them yet?" He wants to know, not needing to explain who he means.

"No," I quietly admit.

"Can I ask why?"

"Anything you want to know, I'll tell you. There's been a lot going on since the ceremony, and I don't just mean with me meeting and falling in love with you."

"Dirty-D and Brittney running in to each other after all these years." I nod, as I'd told him about their situation seeing as how the two men are friends and work together at the station.

"Seems like a few other connections were formed, too."

"That it did. Maybe Tarpley needs a new tourist slogan," he teases.

I volunteer him, stating, "I'll let you come up

with that." I grin, then remind him to keep it PG when he gets this mischievous expression, which turns to mock surprise at my words.

He calls me a spoilsport as he smacks my ass, then gives me a passionate kiss. "Ready to do this?" He questions me, no sign of the nerves remaining. Kevin barks, and I say I agree with him, so we get out, giving Kevin a few minutes to sniff the area. He also marks his territory in quite a few places, thankfully having already done the other so we don't need to clean that up.

When I unlock the door, Tank has Kevin stay by us, then glances around. I offer to give him a tour, then point out what we've restored, letting him know who did what. He seems impressed, which I appreciate as we put a lot into making it livable. We made some good memories here, and I'll treasure those, but it's time for me to make new ones, and I can't really do that here.

Once we're in my room, we assemble the boxes we brought, then begin packing my stuff. It doesn't take long to do as I truly don't have a lot, my childhood teaching me that less is easier to deal with when we needed to move again. When he asks if that's it, I laugh at his surprise, and when I explain why I have so little, he gets sad. I tell him not to, that I enjoyed traveling as I did. "That being said, I'm looking forward to putting down solid roots, gathering knickknacks and stuff to decorate the house."

"You can put up anything you want. I love the idea of knowing you saw something and pictured it in our home. It means you're putting your personal stamp on it."

I tap his cheek, and decide to mess with him. "And if I flooded the place with pink?"

He spins around, as if he's taking in my room and the style with which I'd decorated it. "Yeah, I don't see that being a problem. Besides, I think I've only seen you wear that color two, maybe three times."

"Perhaps that's because I didn't have *my* clothes as I'd only packed for a short visit," I remind him, which leaves him thinking. I'd supplemented it by borrowing from Jemma and ordering online. Honestly, I had needed more outfits, especially with the change of employment, so the latter is something I would've done regardless.

"You could ask me to wear pink and I would," he vows. Hmm...I might just have to. "What about your bed, dresser, and desk?"

"The last two I'd like to keep. The other, that's

up to you." I have no attachment to it whatsoever, I just slept in it, and restlessly at that for the most part. He says it wouldn't be a bad idea to put it in the third bedroom. I agree, so we tear it down, then put it off to the side. As for the dresser and desk, we make sure both are emptied and the stuff that was inside boxed up, then move them to the same spot.

"We'll see what can fit in the trailer without it being too heavy. With them taken apart, we might be able to make it work." If I could see inside his head, I bet there'd be gears turning as he plotted how to squeeze all three inside, seeing it as a challenge to do so. And as if he'd be letting me down if he failed. Something he could never do.

Tank

On one hand, I know this is more for Calliope as she feels it to be the best decision for her, and I'm thankful to be by her side for it. But on the other, I can't help the worry that she'll regret it, and therefore me.

Honestly, it's been on my mind for a while, and perhaps might be why I was so eager to grab her stuff. To my way of thinking, as convoluted as it may be, once her things are in my house, then it's officially *ours* and she won't leave. Ever.

Stupid, I know, but people in love don't always act rationally, especially if they feel their relationship is threatened. I'm kinda glad she finally called me on out. Not like I really hid it well during the drive, or tried to since I wanted to talk about. Needed to.

And now I feel better after having done so. However, I do have one more question. "Why do you have so many books by Lawrence Slater? I thought Bree was his biggest fan." She tries to deflect, making me even more determined to find out the answer. "We packed others, but his are the majority."

"So, um, love means we have a secrecy pact, right?" When I nod, wondering where she's going with this, she adds, "Let's pinky swear." I crack up, remembering my sisters doing that when they were little, terming it 'sister shhh," trying to get something over on me or mom. In their heads, if they did it, neither would get in trouble. Playing along, I raise both pinkies toward her, finding her absolutely precious when she says they'll cancel each other out.

"We can't have that," I say with a smile, and she glances at me, checking to see if I'm being silly, and I am. Then she grins, and I realize I'm not the only one.

"I know the author personally." My eyes narrow, and call it childish, but I'm hoping he's an older man, more of the father or grandfatherly type. Hell, I'd take uncle.

"Go on," I urge, my words probably a bit hard to decipher through gritted teeth.

"I won't prolong it and extend your misery, so I'll start by saying Lawrence isn't his *first* name." I start putting the pieces together then mentally turn them this way and that to see the complete picture. And it clicks into place.

"Of course. It's your brother."

"Yep."

"He can live then," I tell her with benevolence.

She swipes her hand across her forehead, then says, "Phew, I was worried." Her attempt at seriousness is ruined when she not only giggles, but throws one of the decorative pillows at me, and unerringly finds her target.

"Did you leave that out on purpose, just in case

you needed to do that?" I accuse as I edge closer. She reacts as if she's offended, but I see her take a step back, preparing. When I scoop her up in my arms, I point out, "We should've waited on that bed until tomorrow morning."

Threading her fingers through my hair, she gives it a little tug, and informs me with more than a bit of sass, not to mention an obvious taunt, "There are four walls and a floor, I'm sure we can figure something out."

And we did. Twice.

14

CALLIOPE

It's been a week since our trip, and yes, he managed to get all my stuff at the same time. My talk with Brittney after we got back was easy, and she admitted she'd kind of known it was coming for a while, even before I met Tank. That was a relief for me, and the fact Lars and I essentially do the same thing means I'm not leaving the team in a lurch or rushing to replace me.

Now Tank and I are taking a walk around our street, waving at our neighbors, stopping to talk to others, while we enjoy the nice weather. Well, I am, he, however, about has his head on a swivel with the way it's constantly looking from left to right, and even behind me.

When he catches me watching him, his expression becomes innocent, though he doesn't stop inspecting the very air around me. Ahhh. I get it now.

"How long before the bubble arrives?"

"Don't think I didn't contemplate it." The pretense is gone, and he doesn't even attempt to pretend he doesn't know what I'm referring to.

"I don't doubt it. It's your nature to protect those you care for, and I thank you for it."

"For caring?" He seems confused.

"It's sweet. But you do know you can't keep nature away from me, right?"

"Yeah," he grumbles, clearly not happy about that fact.

"You're still gonna try, aren't you?" He doesn't answer, not that he needed to as I already knew before I asked. "While I appreciate it, more than I can express, it's not possible. I take precautions, I have my medicines, and I can't avoid all the triggers. Otherwise, I'd never leave the house, and that's not happening."

"But we could spend it all in bed," he suggests, wagging his brows as his hands slide down to cup my ass and give it a squeeze.

"Awfully cheeky today," I observe, making him chuckle.

"Likewise," he responds, doing it again.

"Wanna know something?" When he says yep, I confess, "You said that when we first met, and it made me all feely."

"Really? A word?"

"I happen to find smart men attractive."

He starts saying things randomly, or so I thought. "Hence. Ergo. Nonetheless. Plethora."

"What are you doing?"

"Consider it foreplay. They're intelligent sounding." Then he waits a second, and wants to know, "Is it working?"

Tank

When she laughs, knowing I'm the reason for it... it's like she's given me the greatest gift, aside from her heart, that is.

Her ring feels as if it's burning a hole in my pocket, I never leave home without it when we're together, never knowing when the perfect moment might present itself. I have no idea what it'll look like, only that I'll know when it happens.

As we finish our stroll, I can't help but wish my dad was here. I know he'd be so happy for me, and I realize the guilt I felt all these years is fading. I can finally accept that it wasn't my fault. It wasn't anybody's. Things happen without rhyme or reason at times. And by continuing to hold on to the assumption that I was to blame was actually dishonoring him because his dying was my focus, not his life.

You would've loved her dad; I think to myself, and as she turns to smile at me, almost as if she heard me, the breeze ruffles her hair.

Call it fanciful, but I swear the wind whispers, "I do, son."

15

TANK

Once more, I know I'm dreaming, but it feels so real. It's summer, I know that in my mind, meaning it should still be light outside as it's only early evening, but the sky is dark.

The wind is so strong the trees are creaking as they bend directions they aren't meant to, rain, no, hail, is hitting my skin with so much force I wouldn't be surprised if it bruises. I hear Calliope calling me, but I can't see her, and her voice seems to be getting further from me with each step I take. I don't know if it's fading on her end or if I'm going the wrong direction.

Regardless, it's terrifying. I turn and head the other way, my feet slapping the pavement harder, faster. Something tells me there's no time to spare, pushing me to hurry, to save her.

Calliope

I can't wake him. I know he's in the midst of a nightmare, his voice has long gone hoarse from shouting my name, begging me to answer him, yet I'm not reaching him. I can't break through the fear he's currently trapped in.

All I can do is hold him, somehow able to slide under him, my back to the headboard, and place his head on my lap. I'd never be able to manage that any other time, but he's thrashed around so much in his sleep I can.

I stroke his sweat soaked hair off his face, the beat of his heart so erratic, so fierce, my hand is rising from the strength of it.

This is the worst it's been since he brought me into his bed. Honestly, I'm getting scared. How long do I let this go on? I'm hesitant to forcefully pull him out of it, fearing what it could do to his mental state, but I don't know what else to do.

His arms are stretched, palm up, like he's using them to guide him. Can he not see in the dream? Is that why he's so freaked out? And why am I a part of it? I thought once he realized how diligent I was about my limitations due to my health issues that the concern would stop manifesting itself in this form, but I was wrong. It's gotten worse, every night he grows more desperate than the one before.

I quietly talk to him, whispering that I'm okay, that I'm here. I tell him how much I love him; about the life we're going to have together. As my voice grows just as strained as his, he opens his eyes, tears falling from the corners, and stares right at me.

"I can't exist without you. I don't want to," he mouths. "Don't leave me." This man, so strong and proud, such a formidable force, but he's the epitome of a gentle giant if you take the time to look past the exterior, the barrier he built to protect himself from feeling too much.

My response is immediate and sincere. "I won't."

"Promise me," he begs.

"I promise."

16

CALLIOPE

"We've got hot, humid air coming from the north and cold and dry from the south. When these collide, it can lead to the formation of tornadoes," the meteorologist states, his expression grim. "The viewing area is currently on watch status, which means there's been no occurrence at this time, however, severe weather is expected and it can produce dangerous conditions. We will continue monitoring this situation and keep you informed as we know more."

That's not good. I have enough experience and knowledge to know what's coming, even if it hasn't been upgraded to an actual warning yet. It will be. I can't deny that my blood is pumping a bit after hearing the local news, but not in the way you'd think. It has nothing to do with wanting to track the storm or chase it. I don't have the urge to call Brittney and join them.

Instead, I want to rush around town and ensure all the residents are prepared. Tank is currently at work and won't be home for a couple hours, so I secure our house as much as I can. There are some things I can't do simply because I don't have the strength to, and I make a mental note to have Tank take care of those.

I'm fully aware nothing may happen, and I hope it doesn't, but the itch at the back of my neck tells me otherwise.

By the time Tank walks in, the weather is the first thing we talk about after sharing a kiss. Kevin is just as eager to see him, sighing after he gets the attention he wants. I inform him what I did, and what he should do, and he handles that while I make dinner for us.

With him not sleeping well lately, we decide to call it a night a lot earlier than normal. Unfortunately, his phone rings not long after we lay down. I don't even need to ask who it is nor listen to his side of the conversation to know why. I can hear the wind outside, see the dark, greenish sky through our window. Things are about to get scary.

Tank is already up and pulling on his clothes, cell held in place by his shoulder. I'm grabbing his stuff as I see it, knowing time is of the essence, and giving it to him. He tells whoever is on the other end that he'll be there in a few minutes, then hangs up.

"Be careful," I urge him, suddenly fearful, and I can't shake it. He gives me a hard kiss, his hands lingering on my hips, our bodies still touching from the waist down as he reluctantly pulls his lips from mine. "I love you." I needed to say it.

Tank stares at me, probably trying to decipher why I'm acting a bit weird, but we both know we can't get into it right now. "I love you, too." Then he pets Kevin and asks him to be a good boy. "Stay safe," he states. "All of our stuff is irreplaceable. You and Kevin are not." I know this, and *he* knows that, but whether my nerves have rubbed off on him or he's reacting to his own, I'm not sure. "I'll contact you as soon as I can. You need me, call. I might not be able to answer, but..." Then he traces my bottom lip with his thumb, touches his left hand to his heart, and walks out the door. I don't follow him, knowing it'll make it worse on us if I do. Tornadoes hit quickly, and thankfully, don't last that long, though it seems to when you're in the midst of it. Unfortunately, a lot of damage can be done in mere minutes.

Shaking off the morose thought, the foreboding, I gather a few supplies then we head to the basement. I say a fervent prayer for protection over Tank and the town of Tarpley. Kevin and I get as comfortable as possible, then I resign myself to waiting, all while wishing for the best.

The whole time we sit there, I'm unable to think about nothing else but what's happening outside and hoping it's over soon. But I can't stop the fear that's whispering in the back of my mind as a lone tear falls...Why did that feel like a good-bye?

Slade

I'd decided to surprise my sister by delivering the books in person instead of mailing them. Plus, I want to see her and meet this Tank. Make sure he's good enough for her, not that I think anyone is.

According to my GPS, I'm not quite two hours away, but I know I have to stop. The sky is dark and dangerous, which means I should take cover just in case. I quickly find shelter and hope it avoids not only the city I'm in, but Tarpley, too.

The second I get the all clear, if my SUV makes it through this, I won't be able to get to Calliope fast enough. My gut is twisting, and it won't stop until I know my sister is okay.

Tank

We did what we could before the tornadoes, yes, plural, hit, and once we knew they were gone and the threat lifted, we emerged from where we'd taken shelter and began to help the residents. Not only of Tarpley, but the surrounding areas as some of us made the short drive to check on them. We're prepared for any possibilities, even as we hope none come to fruition.

My hand reached for my phone at least a dozen

times while we waited, but each was interrupted prior to making contact with it. And now, as we survey the damage and give assistance where needed, I don't even get a chance to try.

News of those who are okay and any that aren't come from word of mouth, relief coursing through me when I learn my mom and Bree are in the former group. I haven't heard anything about Carly yet, making me worry, but I remind myself she could be doing the same thing I am. A few have mentioned seeing Calliope after the storm, saying how sweet it is of her and Kevin to check on them. I thank them for letting me know and their kind words, then move on to help the next person.

My town is not that big nor are there a lot of people, so it doesn't take long before everyone has been seen to, even with me having been sent to Bandera first. I pass a few buildings; some having been hit while others weren't touched. The thing about tornadoes is how random they can be. Two houses could be side by side, and only one get demolished, so you really never know what you might find.

I haven't come across Calliope at all, which is a bit disconcerting as I should have. When I see an unfamiliar SUV with a trailer in back stop not far from where I am and park, I'm curious, of course, but I don't think too much of it. Yet.

That changes when I see the guy who emerged from it stop the Jessups, a couple I've known since I was a kid, and they turn in a circle to look around. When they land on me, both point in my direction and give me a little wave which I return. I've been a man on a mission, so I recognize it in others, and that's exactly what I see as the stranger rapidly makes his way toward me, determination in his face and stride.

"You Tank?" It takes me a second to realize who it is, but there's no denying the resemblance when he gets closer. He tilts his head, tugging on his ear as he waits for me to confirm it. I've seen my Calliope do the same when she's anxious, though she doesn't realize it's one of her tells. Not that I'm going to point it out, either. It gives me a heads up, and sometimes a man needs all the help he can get to understand his woman.

I nod, then hold out my hand. It's dirty, probably has a few scrapes, too, but he shakes it. "Slade, I presume." It's not a question.

He wastes no time on formalities, but gives me a chin lift, then asks, "Where's my sister?" I like that she's his first concern, which isn't unexpected as she's told me how tight they are. Which makes what I have to say next even harder.

"I don't know." I see the swing coming and duck, but it was a diversion tactic, because he's obviously left-handed as that's the punch that lands. And there's some power behind it. Must be that military training she mentioned.

"I know ways to kill that would make your head spin," seeing as he's a writer, I have no doubt his creativity can be scary, "and I will come up with the most painful one to use if you don't fucking find her." But it still will be nowhere near as terrifying as not knowing where she is, nor even where to start looking.

There's no other word for what we do next except interrogation. It doesn't matter who crosses our path, we each ask the same question, "Have you seen Calliope?" Thankfully, everyone knows who she is by now, and she's become part of the Tarpley family. They love her because of who she is, not only due to her being with me.

Jensen Roland, a relative newcomer himself despite living here about five years now, wipes his brow as he'd been moving some of the debris out of the way, and tells us he saw her about thirty minutes ago. "Where at?" I ask, forcing myself not to grab him by the collar and shake the details I need out of him.

"Some were making a list about who hadn't checked in or been seen, so a few offered to go check on them. Callie took the Millner's' place. "

Slade groans, his grumble matching mine and says, "Of course she did."

We start to walk away, intent on getting to her, when Jensen stops us. "Hey, you might want to hurry," he says, voice full of concern.

"Explain," I demand.

"She didn't sound good. I figured she just didn't feel well."

"Why'd you think that?" Slade wants to know.

"Had on one of those medical masks." He wipes the sweat off his forehead before it drips into his eye. "Sure was coughing a lot, seemed like she was having trouble breath…" I'm gone. I don't need to hear the rest of it.

It's my nightmare come to life. I couldn't find her then, but I'll be damned if that's the case now. The storm may have left Tarpley relatively unscathed, but I will destroy it in my quest to get to her if I need to.

"Tank!" Slade hollers, and it takes me a second to realize I'm full out running toward the Millner place, having left him behind. "Why don't you get in and I'll drive us there?" I glare at him, but he has a point, so I stomp toward the passenger door and hop in. "There's something you aren't telling me. You're scared. Why?" He throws a quick glance at me, then returns his eyes to the street and skirts around a dented trash can in the middle of it. "Don't lie to me. It's more than not knowing where she is."

Fuck. This is not how he should be told. I search my side of the road, hoping for another of those signs, trying to delay spilling her secrets, all while knowing he needs to be told. "Where are you, muse."

"Is that a dog?" Slade asks. When I follow his gaze and see Kevin in front of us, I shout his name to which he barks, then jets to the left. "He yours?"

"Yeah."

"Then why did he run away from you?" Good question.

And it takes me longer than it should to answer it, my only excuse being that my mind is so focused on finding my woman. "He didn't. He was running *to* Calliope." Slade doesn't hesitate to turn off the engine and get out. I do the same and try to see where Kevin went. When he gives a bark, this one more urgent, we take off. "This is bad, this is really fucking bad."

"What?"

"I'll tell you what I know, but it's not much," I offer.

"Don't do that," he says. "You and I both know she told you all of it. I appreciate you trying to spare my feelings about her not sharing it with us, but don't downplay what you two have. Okay?"

"All right. Sorry?"

"Don't be. I know why you did it, and it was a thoughtful gesture." I explain everything in as few words as possible, knowing Calliope can go into more detail later, as we continue to follow Kevin.

"She and I are gonna have a chat. Why wouldn't she tell me? Forget that question, I can figure that out on my own. She has asthma now, too?"

I nod, which he probably can't see. "Both are under control, though. She knows what to avoid, and has prescriptions to help combat it, as well as emergency meds if necessary." As Kevin finally stops, he barks rapidly and I glance around, focusing my flashlight on where he's sitting. "And we're going to need those," I add.

The Millners are all about natural remedies, and sell numerous items online and in town. Their main ingredient in the majority of them? Chamomile.

Walking toward Kevin, I fall to my knees when I see her amidst the plants, then aim the beam at her chest. Please, please, please, I beg, praying that I see it rise and fall. But it's not. Jensen mentioned her having trouble when he saw her, and that was with the mask on, which is now missing.

Gently searching her, my hands tremble as I look for the bag she's always wearing. I need it. "We have to locate her purse," I tell her brother, trying to keep my voice steady, keep the fear that's creeping up my throat out of it. "It's yellow, so it should be easy to find," I state, leaving off the part about how it could be anywhere in this field.

"What's going on?" He asks, voice pleading. Poor guy is still trying to wrap his head around his sister's health issues, and now he's about to get an up close and personal example of how they impact her.

"Jensen said she was already having difficulties, and since she lost her mask, the dust, on top of her rushing around, and the severe weather," and probably worried about me, damn it, "more than likely triggered an asthma attack."

"That's not good," he responds quietly.

Take a second to think, Reardon. Fuck! Of course! "Actually, that might be what saves her life." He starts scoping the area closest to us, immediately traipsing after Kevin when he leads him a different direction. While they're doing that, I begin checking Calliope, relying on the little medical training I have, hoping it's enough until we can get her more.

"Kevin, you're getting steak for the rest of your life," Slade shouts as he runs back toward me. "It had gotten stuck on a downed tree," he says, holding out her bag. Taking it, I quickly unzip it and find what I need. Thank god she showed me how to work these things, wanting me to be prepared if I needed to administer one.

"Are you about to jam that in her leg?" He wants to know, incredulously.

"Yes," I answer. "It's the only way." Then I do exactly that, pressing the plunger to get all the medicine in her. I drop it beside me once it's empty, then massage her thigh. I don't know if it's helping her, but it is me. I need to touch her. Grabbing her rescue inhaler, I have it ready just in case she needs it, too.

"I know you're kinda busy here," Slade pipes in, "but I'm losing my mind. Talk to me."

"She had an asthma attack and couldn't get to her inhaler. That means the muscles of her bronchial tube," yeah, I did some research after we talked about this, "constrict, which then makes breathing extremely difficult. Add to that the fact she's highly allergic to chamomile..."

"But she's fucking surrounded by it."

"And she's. Not. Breathing." Piece it together, Lawrence.

"Oh shit. Her lungs were closed."

It seems like it's been hours since I gave her the injection, but it hasn't been more than a minute tops. "You promised, muse," I remind her, laying my head on her chest, wanting to hear that first breath she takes. When she does, I can finally take one of my own.

"Stuck me, Sherman," Calliope whispers.

"Now I know how your parents felt when they first heard you cry," I tell her, tears pouring down my cheeks. She tries to sit up, but I force her to wait.

"Not yet, sweetheart. Let the medicine do its job first."

"Your arms," she says, voice only a smidge stronger, but I'll take it.

I smile at her, then ask, "You want me to hold

you?" I'm already stretching out beside her and slowly pulling her against me. When she sighs, her head nestled on my shoulder, the feeling of her breath gliding over my skin... "This is a moment," I say softly in her ear, knowing she'll understand what I mean.

"One of many for us," she predicts, the number of words that time easing my worry because it lets me know the meds are kicking in. It's quiet for a few minutes, but I know Slade is bursting at the seams to check on her.

"Your brother is here," I inform her. "As much as I don't want to let you go, he needs to hug you, too. Can you stand up? Never mind." I reposition myself, now hunched over as if I'm doing squats, then lift her and straighten.

"That's pretty sexy," she tells me.

"Can you not when I can hear you?" Slade asks gruffly, but I can hear the relief in it.

"Let's get her to the hospital," I suggest, "then you can talk after she sees a doctor." I have him pick up the used injector and put the cap back on it before returning it to her bag. I don't know if they'll need it, so I want to have it on the off chance they do. He leads the way back to his SUV, the engine still running as we'd been in too much of a hurry for him to pay it any mind. He opens the back door so I can slide in without disturbing her, and Kevin hops in beside me and we're rushing toward help the instant Slade gets behind the wheel.

17

CALLIOPE

"Dad, Mom, she's fine. I swear. You don't have to…" I hear what sounds like my brother saying to the right of me, but that can't be possible. "Okay, we'll see you in a few days."

"So, I'll be meeting my future in-laws soon," Tank states, and I catch the laughter in his tone. Slade, and yes, it really is him, is not amused.

"You aren't engaged yet, asshole."

"My ring on her finger says otherwise." What now? I try to raise my left hand, the movement taking way too much energy, and instead attempt to lift my head to look. Nope. That's not working either. Plan c, I contort my fingers so I can touch the area in question and sure enough, there it is.

"Do over. I need that moment," I say, not sure if

they can even hear me. I shouldn't have worried, though, as both of them immediately turn toward me.

"About time you joined us, brat. The things you do for attention," Slade teases.

"You scared me," Tank tells me as he leans down to kiss me.

"I kept my promise," I remind him.

"And that ring is one from me. I promise to love you until my last breath, and into the hereafter. I will never make you regret tying your life to mine. I will support you no matter what you do. I will take care of you when you're sick, and try not to drive you nuts when I am." I laugh through my tears at the last part.

"I came to Tarpley in search of a home, a future." I work my arms up to cup his cheeks, thankful using them is getting easier. "I never expected to find both in a person. I thought a home had to be a building, a future a new job, and while they can be and are in a way, I know where I belong…forever."

"And where's that?" He wants to know, his voice deep with emotions.

Utterly confident in my declaration, I say, "With you."

"Will you marry me, Calliope Anna Lawrence?"

I nod, my throat too clogged with tears to answer."

"Give me the word, baby.

"Yes."

* * *

We're home now, the doctor discharging me after running a few tests, and Kevin hasn't left my side. He's been given lots of love and treats to thank him for watching over me and getting me help, but I know that's not the reason why.

Tank has barely taken his eyes off me, or let me out of reach. In fact, I'm on his lap right now, not that I'm complaining. I feel as if I can't get close enough to him. He and Slade explained where they found me, and how, so I'll have to bake Jensen a cake or something. Or maybe buy it, since I'm trying to show appreciation, not hurt him.

Cooking, no problem. Baking? They might try to arrest me, citing intent to harm. I made Slade cookies once for his birthday and he asked, "What did I ever do to you?" I now threaten to do it again when he's being a brat.

"You know," Slade says about an hour later, "you had breathing problems years ago."

"She never mentioned that," Tank states.

"I didn't know," I tell him.

"You were young. Hell, so was I. But I was old enough to remember feeling helpless, running to Mom crying, begging her to fix you. They eventually faded, as the doctor predicted they might. Dad and Mom thought that was the end of it."

"And it was, until I got stung."

"If it hadn't been so many times…"

"All that venom, and the mosquito bites on top of it, my system was overloaded."

"And restarted those earlier struggles into full-blown asthma."

"What you're telling me," Tank begins, "is my woman likes to bring up the past?" I turn to find him smothering a laugh, which becomes an "oomph," when I elbow him in the side. "I'm teasing, baby." I can't even be mad, not that I was, because his eyes are twinkling, the haunted look that's been in them for weeks due to his dreams is gone.

"Maybe you aren't that bad after all," I hear Slade mutter as he leaves the living area, giving Tank and I privacy. He's not going far as we offered him one of our guest rooms.

"You're growing on him," I inform Tank with a smile.

"Like a fungus," Slade pipes in as he walks upstairs, his chuckle lingering after he disappears from sight.

Tank stands, once more his strength surprising me, and calls Kevin as we head to our room. We don't make love, but we don't need to in order to feel close. We're in our bed, arms wrapped around each other, his ring on my finger, hearts beating in sync.

"Did you know the earliest rings are reported to be from Ancient Egypt?" He chuckles, and I join him when he tells me that he visualized me doing this in one of his good dreams. "They were more than likely braided together with hemp or reeds."

"Why are they worn on the left?" He asks, confident I know. And I do.

"Romans were of the mind the vein in that finger had a direct route to the heart.

"I hope are kids are just like you," he murmurs against my hair as we fall asleep, not stirring until my alarm goes off, surprising us both as Tank's internal clock didn't wake him. Neither did his nightmare.

18

TANK

Life is good, great, perfect. All the words I can think of to describe how wonderful the past couple weeks have been. Calliope has fully recovered, and promised she'll never go near the Millners' property again unless it's the offseason for their crop. They harvest in the fall, so when spring and summer hit, it's in full-bloom, a perk of warm weather year-round. Unfortunately, that's when she was there.

I haven't dreamed since that night Slade and I saved Calliope. Our theory is I was having them because fate knew she was mine, even though we hadn't met yet. And when we did, they served as a warning, reminding me every minute counts. That we must cherish those we're given, not to waste any. If I had, she might not be with me today.

The doctor told us if she'd gone without air for much longer, but Slade and I had stopped him right there, not wanting him to finish that sentence. As if speaking those horrible words could turn back time and make them come true.

Today is Bree's birthday party, and we're gathered at Mom's house, waiting for Bree to blow out the candles. Slade wasn't able to stay, but he'll be returning soon. He's decided to live here, wanting to be near his sister, and the nephews and nieces he said he can't wait to start spoiling. He'd confessed he'd hand delivered the signed books in order to make sure I was worthy of her, and when I told him I knew I wasn't; he'd welcomed me to the family. He also, which Calliope informed me meant he truly liked me, left his bike with us so he wouldn't have to worry about it during the move.

An hour later, Bree starts opening her presents, and the one from Calliope, though she'd written my name on it, too, is the only gift remaining.

When she unwraps it, her scream has me covering my ears. I knew she'd enjoy it, but I may have underestimated how much. She asks how as she looks through the books, to which my fiancée whispers, "I know people," but Bree's question is forgotten as she reaches the bottom. Slade included his newest, which won't be released until August, making Calliope and now Bree the only two that have printed copies so far.

Bree gives her the biggest hug, and tells her thank you. Calliope, as do myself and the others, assume Bree is referring to the hardcovers, but she's not. "No," Bree corrects her when she says she knows she'll give them a good home, "though I appreciate them very much. I meant for loving my brother. You brought him back to life, and that's the greatest gift you could've ever given our family."

EPILOGUE

Calliope

Five years later…

"I'll see you Monday. Have a good weekend," I tell my class right before the bell rings.

They gather their things, eagerly heading to the door and freedom, but they all stop to say, "Bye, Mrs. Reardon." That name never fails to make me smile, nor to be thankful for the path my life has taken since visiting Tarpley.

I was so lost before Jemma unintentionally gave

me that olive branch, neither of us knowing how deeply accepting it would impact me. It changed everything for me, and I will never be able to repay her for that, even if she repeatedly tells me I don't need to. Not that it stops me from trying.

She and Angel got married two months after the tornado hit, and you could not only see, but also feel the love between them as they said their vows. I was honored when she asked me to be her maid of honor, and thankful when she agreed to stand with me at my own.

Tank and I didn't want a long engagement, nor a big wedding, so we kept it simple by inviting those closest to us, the whole town, our families, and friends, to join us for a short but sweet ceremony. Afterwards, we celebrated with a picnic, our guests eagerly offering to bring dishes to feed everyone. We played games, had a bonfire, and made s'mores. It was perfect. The next morning, he surprised me by whisking me off for a weekend getaway. The cabin was beautiful, and so was the location…the little we saw of it as we hardly left the bedroom.

Not only did Slade make the move, our parents did, too. Their houses aren't far from ours, so we see each other a lot, not that it's hard to do being such a small town and close-knit community. Slade and Tank have become good friends, though they still poke at each other any chance they get. They even work together when needed as Slade became a volunteer firefighter. It's actually the perfect job for him as he works from home due to his writing, and when they get a call, it gives him the adrenaline burst I know he misses since leaving the military.

He's also a family man now, and he took to it like a natural. Not that I had any doubts. My brother is a good man, and I'm not the only one who thinks so.

Bree is doing great. On a whim, she'd decided to learn how to create and maintain websites. When I asked Tank about it, thinking it quite random, he said she's always been like that, routinely seeking a challenge. She discovered she enjoyed it, and started by creating a couple for local businesses, then branched out to offering her services online. The constant variety of it appeals to her, but having a desk across from her husband's in their home office is her favorite part. Well, that and both of them being there for their daughter. My niece is the cutest little girl, and I dare anyone to disagree.

Dad and Mom have retired, though they help from time to time at the various schools around us. They love being grandparents, as does Lorna, and have informed their children they want more to spoil. They're getting their wish; they just don't know it yet.

Tomorrow, we're having a barbecue, and we plan on announcing that we're pregnant with our second child. We currently have a son, Otto. He's almost four and the spitting image of his father, and the grandfather he'll never get a chance to meet. He will, however, know *of* him.

Tank has been sharing stories of our son's namesake, and we have a few pictures around the house, as does nana, as Otto calls Lorna, and his aunts. When he passes by one of the photos, he kisses his left ring finger, touches the image of his pop-pop, and, depending on his mood that day, either says, hi, I love you, or I miss you. We aren't sure where it came from, he just started doing it. Our theory is that he's heard us greet each other like that after being apart due to work or whatever reason. I fully believe children are emotionally intuitive, and this is how he chooses to have a bond with him. When he visits his daddy at the shop, he gets a kick out of seeing his name on the sign and talks about being a "vroom man," as he refers to Tank's job. It's so cute that we don't correct him with the actual name for it.

He'll eventually outgrow some of it, and begin using the right term, but until then, we'll cherish the connection he's forged in his own adorable way and his Otto speak.

As I drive home, the scenery never fails to take my breath, which makes me smile. It's a silly play on words considering, but I can't resist. Tank is finally at the point where he can laugh with me about it, realizing it's a type of coping for me.

He's still just as vigilante in keeping triggers away from me whenever possible, and ensures that any product that comes into our home doesn't contain chamomile. Some might find it stifling, but it's actually very sweet. He loves me, unconditionally, and his actions show it.

And the way he looks at me when I walk in the door, his eyes devouring me, heat barely banked in their depths, tells me when we take to our bed in a few hours, he's going to do so again and again. Actions truly can speak louder than words. But sometimes, as he proves following the demonstration of what I do to him, they're just as wonderful.

* * *

Later that night, our bodies sweaty from making love, Tank places his hand on my belly to cradle our unborn child, and tells me of his latest dream. They're no longer premonitions bad is coming, but something good. "We have a girl with your black hair and my green eyes."

"What do we name her?" I ask, already in love with her as is he.

"Hope," he says, and I know instantly that's what it will be.

Epilogue Two
Tank

Ten years after meeting…

"Dad?" Otto, in his cute nine-year-old voice, calls out from beside me.

"Yeah, son?"

"I need a wrench," he informs me. We're currently under my truck as I'm changing the breaks, and he's "helping" me. His overalls are a miniature version of the ones I wear at the garage, and his name is on the pocket, just like mine have Tank.

"Skewdiver," Hope chimes in, correcting him. She is not under the car, of course, as she's only four, but watching from her mommy's lap. Kevin is at their side, his ears perking when she speaks. It's pretty much the only tool she remembers, and she seems to like saying it, so she always mentions it, regardless of the job at hand.

However, I'm a sucker for my family, so I grab it and pretend to use it, my heart swelling with love as she cheers. Just as it does when I make my wife smile, or our son laugh.

It's my mission to do whatever I can to make my wife and our children happy. They are the light of my life and bring me nothing but joy.

Calliope is still teaching, though she now does so at a school in Medina. I don't work as many hours at the shop, preferring to spend as much at home as possible. I'm always here by the time she and the kids walk in the door, and sometimes I even pick them up myself, wanting to hear all about their day as soon as I can.

I haven't quit the department, but I have been contemplating it. I'm getting older, my reflexes not as quick as they could be, however, Calliope knew

I wasn't ready to yet. She wants to make sure when I do step down it's because it's what I want, not for any other reason. And that time is coming, I know it, and I'm okay with it.

Over the years, we've come to know the other better than we do ourselves. When her asthma wakes her during the night, I'm already sitting up, inhaler in hand, somehow knowing before her that it's coming. And when her breathing is once again stabilized, she understands when I lay my head on her chest, knowing while she may have calmed down, her heart beating under my ear is what will help me do the same.

Because her voice isn't the only beautiful sound she makes.

Stay tuned. You never know what this crew will get up to in the future. *wink*

Thank you for reading FIGHTING FOR CLLIOPE! I hope you enjoyed the experience. Be sure to check out the other books in this exciting miniseries, all set in Susan Stoker's Badge of Honor world. The men—and women—of the Tarpley VFD are ready to fight for their lives and their loves. The books are all standalone stories though they share some characters and events. The suggested reading order is:

#1 **Fighting for Elena** by Silver James – Pops and Elena

#2 **Fighting for Carly** by Deanndra Hall – Dub-step and Carly

#3 **Fighting for Calliope** by Haven Rose – Tank and Callie

#4 Fighting for Jemma by MJ Nightingale – Short Shit and Jemma

#5 Fighting for Brittney by TL Reeve – Dirty-D and Brittney

#6 Fighting for Nadia by Nicole Flockton – Buff and Nadia

Look for all the other books in Susan Stoker's Worlds at www.acespress.com.

*

If you liked Tank and Callie's story, please take a moment to leave a review. Not only are authors happy to know they've brought enjoyment to someone's life by providing an escape from reality, even if only for a short time, but they are a way for others to decide if they'd also be interested. The greatest way to share your love for their work is by word of mouth, whether it's literally, or through your own written word in a review.

ABOUT THE AUTHOR

Haven Rose spends her days high atop the world in a tower overlooking a beautiful meadow, waiting for her prince to find her. No? That's a different story? Okay. In real life, the author, who prefers to remain a mystery, met her true love at a very young age and the two have been enjoying their lives together ever since. Has it had its ups and downs? Yes, but their love for one another has endured it all and only grown stronger. He is the foundation upon which her Heroes are created. She knows things can never be perfect in a relationship, at least not outside of books, which is why the pen name of Haven Rose was created, allowing readers, such as herself, to escape into a world where problems are easily solved, love is instant and true, and the story is always safe.

Stay Connected

You can email the author, if you'd like, at

havenroseauthor@gmail.com. Haven has created a Facebook page for those interested in connecting with her or for updates on current works in progress and future books. That link is - https://www.facebook.com/authorhavenrose/. You can also follow her author page or on BookBub (bookbub.com/authors/haven-rose). While she does not currently have a website, she has created a closed reader group on Facebook. If you're interested in becoming a member, please visit The Rose Garden at facebook.com/groups/227103614772999/.

Thank you for taking the time to meet this couple, and those near and dear to them, as well as characters you may see in future books.

Tarpley VFD Series

Fighting for Calliope

Accidental Connection Series

The Hopeful Heart

The Enduring Heart

Matter of Hart Series

That Day

Getting Lucky

Love's Draw

Love for the Holidays Series

Sweet Surprise

Mistletoe Magic

A Tangled Wed Series

Grave Secrets

Lethal Memories

Final Truth

Holidays in Jasper Series

Trick or Treat

Thankfully Yours

Merry New Year

From The Heart

Shamrocked

His Firecracker

Summer's End

Other Books

Love's Valley Duet

Pieces of You

A Home for Noelle

Rule Breaker

Seduced by a Whisper

There are many more books in this fan fiction world than listed here, for an up-to-date list go to www.AcesPress.com

You can also visit our Amazon page at: http://www.amazon.com/author/operationalpha

Special Forces: Operation Alpha World

Christie Adams: Charity's Heart
Denise Agnew: Dangerous to Hold
Shauna Allen: Awakening Aubrey
Brynne Asher: Blackburn
Linzi Baxter: Unlocking Dreams
Jennifer Becker: Hiding Catherine
Heather Blair: Rescue Me
Anna Blakely: Rescuing Gracelynn
Julia Bright: Saving Lorelei
Victoria Bright: Surviving Savage
Cara Carnes: Protecting Mari
Kendra Mei Chailyn: Beast
Melissa Kay Clarke: Rescuing Annabeth
Samantha A. Cole: Handling Haven
Sue Coletta: Hacked
Melissa Combs: Gallant
KaLyn Cooper: Rescuing Melina

Sarah Curtis: Securing the Odds
Jordan Dane: Redemption for Avery
Tarina Deaton: Found in the Lost
KL Donn: Unraveling Love
Riley Edwards: Protecting Olivia
PJ Fiala: Defending Sophie
Nicole Flockton: Protecting Maria
Michele Gwynn: Rescuing Emma
Casey Hagen: Shielding Nebraska
EM Hayes: Gambling for Ashleigh
Desiree Holt: Protecting Maddie
Kathy Ivan: Saving Sarah
Jesse Jacobson: Protecting Honor
Silver James: Rescue Moon
Becca Jameson: Saving Sofia
Kate Kinsley: Protecting Ava
Heather Long: Securing Arizona
Kirsten Lynn: Joining Forces for Jesse
Margaret Madigan: Bang for the Buck
Kimberly McGath: The Predecessor
Rachel McNeely: The SEAL's Surprise Baby
KD Michaels: Saving Laura
Wren Michaels: The Fox & The Hound
Kat Mizera: Protecting Bobbi
Mary B Moore: Force Protection
LeTeisha Newton: Protecting Butterfly

Angela Nicole: Protecting the Donna
MJ Nightingale: Protecting Beauty
Sarah O'Rourke: Saving Liberty
Anne L. Parks: Mason
Debra Parmley: Protecting Pippa
Lainey Reese: Protecting New York
TL Reeve and Michele Ryan: Extracting Mateo
Elena M. Reyes: Keeping Ava
Angela Rush: Charlotte
Rose Smith: Saving Satin
Jenika Snow: Protecting Lily
Lynn St. James: SEAL's Spitfire
Dee Stewart: Conner
Harley Stone: Rescuing Mercy
Jen Talty: Burning Desire
Megan Vernon: Protecting Us

Police and Fire: Operation Alpha World

Freya Barker: Burning for Autumn
KaLyn Cooper: Justice for Gwen
Aspen Drake: Sheltering Emma
Deanndra Hall: Shelter for Sharla
Barb Han: Kace
CM Steele: Guarding Hope
Reina Torres: Justice for Sloane
Stacey Wilk: Stage Fright

As you know, this book included at least one character from Susan Stoker's books. To check out more, see below.

SEAL of Protection: Legacy Series

Securing Caite

Securing Brenae (novella)

Securing Sidney

Securing Piper

Securing Zoey

Securing Avery (May 2020)

Securing Kalee (Sept 2020)

Delta Team Two Series

Shielding Gillian (Apr 2020)

Shielding Kinley (Aug 2020)

Shielding Aspen (Oct 2020)

Shielding Riley (TBA)

Shielding Devyn (TBA)

Shielding Ember (TBA)

Shielding Sierra (TBA)

Delta Force Heroes Series

Rescuing Rayne (FREE!)

Rescuing Aimee (novella)

Rescuing Emily

Rescuing Harley

Marrying Emily (novella)

Rescuing Kassie

Rescuing Bryn

Rescuing Casey

Rescuing Sadie (novella)

Rescuing Wendy

Rescuing Mary

Rescuing Macie (Novella)

Badge of Honor: Texas Heroes Series

Justice for Mackenzie (FREE!)

Justice for Mickie

Justice for Corrie

Justice for Laine (novella)

Shelter for Elizabeth

Justice for Boone

Shelter for Adeline

Shelter for Sophie

Justice for Erin

Justice for Milena

Shelter for Blythe

Justice for Hope

Shelter for Quinn
Shelter for Koren
Shelter for Penelope

SEAL of Protection Series

Protecting Caroline (FREE!)
Protecting Alabama
Protecting Fiona
Marrying Caroline (novella)
Protecting Summer
Protecting Cheyenne
Protecting Jessyka
Protecting Julie (novella)
Protecting Melody
Protecting the Future
Protecting Kiera (novella)
Protecting Alabama's Kids (novella)
Protecting Dakota

New York Times, USA Today and *Wall Street Journal* Bestselling Author Susan Stoker has a heart as big as the state of Tennessee where she lives, but this all American girl has also spent the last fourteen years living in Missouri, California, Colorado, Indiana, and Texas. She's married to a retired

Army man who now gets to follow *her* around the country.

www.stokeraces.com
www.AcesPress.com
susan@stokeraces.com

Made in the USA
Monee, IL
18 February 2020